GW00470721

THE RIVER LINE

Charles Morgan was born in Kent on 22 January, 1894. He died on 6 February, 1958. Educated from boyhood as a naval officer, he served in the Atlantic and the China Fleets. (His experiences as a midshipman gave rise to his first novel, *The Gunroom*.) After service with the Naval Brigade at Antwerp in 1914, he was a prisoner of war for four years. In 1919 he went to Oxford, where he took Honours in Modern History and was President of the Oxford University Dramatic Society. In 1921 he joined the editorial staff of *The Times*, and from 1926 until 1939 was principal dramatic critic to that newspaper. Meanwhile, his novels began to appear. *Portrait in a Mirror* (1929) and *The Fountain* (1932) were followed by *Sparkenbroke*, *The Voyage*, *The Empty Room*, *The Judge's Story*, *The River Line*, and *A Breeze of Morning*. They won for the author three literary prizes, the Femina, the Hawthornden, and the James Tait Black. His play, *The Flashing Stream*, ran for six months in London and for fourteen months in Paris. His second play, *The River Line*, was first produced at the Edinburgh Festival in 1952 before beginning a successful run in London. His third play, *The Burning Glass*, was also widely acclaimed.

He was M.A. of Oxford, Hon. LL.D. of St Andrews, Hon. Doctor of the University of Caen, an Officer of the Legion of Honour and a Member of the Institut de France. The manuscript of his *Ode to France* is preserved in the Bibliothèque Nationale.

THE RIVER LINE

BY

CHARLES MORGAN

First published in Great Britain in 1949. This edition published in 1988 by Robson Books Ltd, Bolsover House, 5-6 Clipstone Street, London W1P 7EB.

British Library Cataloguing in Publication Data

Morgan, Charles, *1894-1958*
The river line.
I. Title
823'.912 F

ISBN 0-86051-485-4
ISBN 0-86051-512-5 Pbk

Printed and bound in Great Britain by
Biddles Ltd., Guildford and King's Lynn

TO

ROGER MORGAN

HIS FATHER DEDICATES

THIS BOOK

1

As his train from London approached Kemble, only the impassivity of his English fellow-passengers kept Sturgess silent. This was the last stage of a long journey from America, and what he would find at the end of it had been the principal reason for his having come. He wanted to rejoice with someone. Happily expectant, he would have liked to express his happiness in friendly talk — with anyone, about almost anything.

Instead, he smiled to himself and said nothing. First as a boy when his father had held a diplomatic post, then as a young man in time of war, he had spent in England too many of his thirty years to think the silence unfriendly. These British would have helped him soon enough if he had needed help. They were untalkative in trains because not to butt in was one of their forms of politeness. They left you alone because it was their way of respecting your privacy. So there they had sat for over two hours behind their books and newspapers, like the stones of Stonehenge.

Sturgess, having a warm heart, gave them credit for good intentions, and beamed upon them, without knowing it, like a boy on holiday. A lady with a tired face, who, he guessed, was more than seventy years old, made him aware that he had been smiling by a tilt of her eyebrows which evidently said: Now what on earth has he found to smile at? Then, observing that he was an American, she smiled back, and returned to her cross-word puzzle. He liked her for that, and wondered whose mother she was and what she had been through that had drawn such fine lines about her mouth and unflinching eyes.

So much had happened since he had last seen Julian Wyburton, and so much more since he and Julian had parted from Marie in France, that he was burning with eagerness for the sound of their voices, the grasp of their hands. Thinking that the train had begun to slow, he took his baggage down from the rack and thrust his head and shoulders through the open window. Julian Wyburton wouldn't say much at first, though Marie, being French, might say more. Then, suddenly, and with a shock of understanding that sent a tremor of fear through the contracting muscles of his arms, he grasped for the first time that Marie, having been a prisoner in the German camp of Ravensbrück, must have changed in appearance. No woman could suffer what she had suffered and not be changed. So powerful was his revulsion from the thought of pain, that he shut his eyes; then, as the train came into Kemble, opened them again and searched the upturned faces.

Neither Marie nor Julian had come to meet him. He stood on the platform momentarily at a loss; then noticed that the elderly lady who had smiled at him was getting out and helped her with her case. "Thank you," she said. "it's really very light. I always manage it myself." She nodded at his Cunard labels. "I see you have come a long way."

"Yes," he said. "I've come to visit some old friends."

But she did not ask about his friends. "Well," she said, "I hope you have a very happy time in England. It isn't an easy country nowadays, I'm afraid."

When she was gone, an old man with a coachman's leathery face came up to ask whether he was the American gentleman going to Mr. Wyburton's at Tarryford. "Mr

Wyburton he's sorry. He was startin' over to meet you isself when a tyre went, an' the spare went yesterday so he phones down to me. That's how 'tis nowadays. Can't get no new tyres for love or money."

Sturgess and the old man carried out the baggage between them and ground their way gingerly through the traffic of Kemble. Outside the town, machine and driver took heart and advanced with greater confidence.

2

THOUGH he had been looking forward so long and eagerly to the moment of his arrival and had imagined it in detail a hundred times, Sturgess was not made impatient by the slowness of the drive. He was glad to have time to re-order his thought. Always he had pictured Marie as she had been four years ago in France, and this, he now perceived, had been unimaginative foolishness.

In the first place, if her appearance had been blotted or maimed by torture, everything was affected, particularly her marriage to Julian Wyburton. After the war, Julian had visited her in a Swiss hospital, brought her to England and married her. The news of that marriage in the summer of Forty-six, almost a year ago now, had astonished Sturgess when he had received it in America. It wasn't a marriage that had ever entered his mind as being likely; moreover, there was, he should have supposed, a bar to it. The thought of Heron must hang between them, for Marie, he would swear, had been in a fair way to loving Heron. Presumably she and Julian had surmounted that difficulty. He was glad that they had, as he was glad of anything that promised happiness to two people he cared for in this entangled world.

He was glad, too, for his own sake. Their marriage, and the fact that Marie had urged him to spend a part of the summer with them, renewed, in conditions of rare intimacy, the comradeship of " his adventure " which, in

France, he had shared with them; and ugly though that adventure had been in one respect — ugly enough to leave a scar upon his memory — he didn't wish to forget it. Not that he wanted life always to run at as high a tension as that, but he was glad that it had once, and that he had not failed in his part. The more he reflected that henceforth his own life, as head of the English Department in Stanley College and perhaps later at Harvard, would be peaceful and scholarly, the better pleased he was to carry within him an experience so violent. It would save him from ever becoming complacent or drily scholastic, if only he could learn to apply it rightly, and he had promised himself that this visit to Julian and Marie should teach as well as delight him. It was to be the happy epilogue to a tragedy; a proof, if they could talk about it calmly in a sane world, that the world was in fact sane; evidence, too, that, with the tragic circumstances safely in the past, the comradeship begotten in stress, the closest he had ever known, remained.

For him, that comradeship shone. He didn't want it dulled or blotted, as it would be if, in his hosts' marriage, some abnormal or tragic quality persisted. No doubt they could "take it"; they would be stubbornly uncomplaining; but this will of the English and the French to endure and endure and endure seemed to him, though he admired it in a way, essentially false, a stoical attitude towards life that was, at root, wrong. When suffering came, you had to face it; but then you snapped out of it as you did out of an illness. It was abnormal, like the light's going out in a room; you groped about a bit, then put in a new fuse, and switched the light on again. What he principally dreaded was that, if Marie had been terribly hurt, the past, the adventure they had shared, would not stay in the area of reminiscence where he liked it to be, but would break through into the present. The happy epilogue would be spoiled.

This working of his own mind perturbed him. It looked like selfishness, and yet he knew that he was not a selfish man. There was nothing he wouldn't do to spare Julian and Marie suffering. The real trouble with me, he reflected, is that, like many other amateur soldiers, I'm in danger of romanticizing my bit of active service. Uncle Toby and Madame Bovary rolled into one. . . . The incongruity of that thought, in association with his scholastic self, so tickled him that he gave a short bark of laughter and followed it with a deep chuckle that anyone but the astonished driver might have found altogether charming. Then, observing the effect he had produced, he blinked away the laughter from his eyes, and wrote " Toby-Bovary " in a crimson note-book taken from his waistcoat pocket and closed the note-book with a snap.

But it's really true, he thought, that I shall have to be on my guard or I shall become an old campaigner who is always talking of battles long ago! He wondered how often he had bored people at home with what he called " the River Line episode ". Maybe you know about the River Line? he heard his own voice begin. It was an organization, you know, run by the Belgians and the French, for helping our airmen — British as well as American — to get home after they'd been shot down in enemy-occupied territory. I was one of them. We were passed on, three of us, from post to post, through Belgium, through France, into Spain — home that way. Sometimes it was a farm, sometimes a wine-cellar we stopped in; sometimes a hut in a disused quarry. On the way south — it was the last lap before the Spanish frontier — at a place called Blaise, there was this girl Marie in charge of us. Marie Chassaigne — daughter of the poet, Pierre

Chassaigne. We lay up in her father's house outside the town. There were just three of us at first — a boy called Frewer, and a fellow with long thin legs that we called Heron though he said his name was Lang, and myself. One night Marie brought in another Britisher, Wyburton. That made five, counting Marie. There was some hitch in the outside plans and we were longer there than anywhere else. We came to know one another, and her, pretty well. And then, on the night we were to start—

I must keep a watch on myself, Sturgess thought, I've told that story too often. It troubled him that he had never been able to tell it as he wished. The facts, yes, and the climax of extreme decision, of violent action, but these were meaningless unless you felt the unity of that little group of five — unless you shared his sense of their having been bound together then and of their being bound together still. Not only the survivors, Julian, Marie and himself, but all five, the dead and the living, still bound together in spite of what had happened — or because of it. He had never been able to make any listener understand that.

"That's where the house lies," the driver said. "No, you can't see it from here, sir, but it lies close in under them trees on the hill yonder."

They were coming downhill into a village, and Sturgess, banishing reminiscence from his nimble mind, sat up to enjoy the present, and straightened his tie. He was delighted to see that, in contrast with the shabby, dispirited towns, this part of England looked so well. The fields at least were smiling in the July sun, the houses of Cotswold stone were undamaged, and, as the car rose to the narrow hump-bridge in Tarryford, Sturgess, seeing below him the small, slow river, asked that they should stop. He jumped out and leaned on the parapet. A pair of swans, as still as the celluloid swans that you floated in a bath, allowed themselves to drift downstream. Two ancient row-boats, tied up to a ring, received on their shadowed sides the thrown-up ripple of water-light. Vintage boats, he thought, and brought out his crimson note-book to record their names: Dreadnought and Princess Ena. The *Dreadnought*, no doubt, had been a battleship, but who was the princess?

In the car again, he asked the driver. "She were a granddaughter o' the Queen's, sir," the old man answered. The ensuing silence was devoted, Sturgess felt, to the glories of the Victorian age, and he did not interrupt it.

3

THE Wyburtons' house was, in a sense, familiar to him, for in France and afterwards in England Julian Wyburton had often spoken of it with affection. A farm two hundred years ago, and preserving still the name of Stanning Farm, it had been reconstructed at the end of the eighteenth century to serve as dower-house to the estate of Tarryford Park. Julian's parents, unable to maintain Tarryford, had moved during his infancy to Stanning and had found it uncomfortably small. He, who had inherited it at his mother's death in 1944, found it, he had lately written, " quite large enough for a working farmer and the devil's own job for Marie to run ! " Sturgess had grinned at that, and, observing the exclamation mark, had guessed that Julian had grinned while he wrote it. Women of the French middle-class weren't afraid of housework, and Marie, as he and Julian had good reason to know, could run anything. Still, he was uncertain whether Julian's determination to farm Stanning himself was successful or not ; they might be struggling ; if so, the struggle would be keen and competent. " Don't be afraid of being a tiresome guest. Stay as long as you will. We shall make you work, I expect," Marie had said in her invitation. " This being a farm, we have some kinds of food, and wood for the winter."

Approaching the house from behind through a wooded lane, the car turned unexpectedly into a sweep bounded by a low parapet of stone, and drew up. Sturgess, climbing out, glanced first at the steeply falling country and the wide view beyond the parapet, then at the house itself, compact and, he felt, welcoming, with its small, stone-pillared porch.

While his baggage was being handed out, he heard a door open behind him and turned.

" Well," he exclaimed warmly, his tone gathering in the past, " this *is* a change ! " and he took the hand Julian stretched out to him, and pressed and held it.

" Good," Julian said. " Glad you've come. Sorry we didn't meet you, Philip. Tyre went at the last moment. But you will have been told that sad story."

As they went up the steps together, Sturgess linked his arm in his host's, but Julian released it to take a case from the driver and carry it into the hall. He was wearing a blue cotton shirt with its sleeves rolled up over slim powerful forearms, a pair of khaki drill trousers, and brown shoes very old and very good. Weathered, lithe and bony, with a neat precision of movement, there was, Sturgess had always thought, something of the Indian about him — a resemblance of poise rather than of feature, for he had light hair sweeping back from a domed forehead and light blue eyes. Now he busied himself with the baggage, throwing over his shoulder a joke about the magnificence of it ; then turned to Sturgess again and asked about his voyage and his journey from London in a way that made him feel a welcome, but not, with any reference to the past, a special guest. But the English, he reflected, often spoke least of what they felt most ; they made almost a vice of avoiding the obvious sentiments of greeting ; and, after all, what had he expected ? — that Julian should throw his arms round his neck ? Julian had been a naval officer ; it wasn't his habit to throw his arms round anyone's neck.

A short fat man in an alpaca jacket now came forward with a slow, wavering step over the stone flags of the hall, and observed the baggage with consternation.

"Did I ought . . . to be beginning to take . . . all these up to the gentleman's room ?" he asked with a long pause after each group of words; then, gazing owl-like through steel-rimmed spectacles, he added with a kind of hopeful hopelessness: "Or wasn't they all ready yet ?"

"Yes," said Julian, "you might make a beginning, Tucker. We'll bring some with us as we come. . . . Look, Philip. This is Tucker. He'll do everything for you if you give him time." Sturgess said cheerfully that he'd look forward to that, and Tucker's welcoming grin made it clear that this was a visitor of whom he approved.

"And now," said Julian, "before I take you up, the first thing after a journey is a drink. There'll be tea soon, but meanwhile—"

He led the way into a small, two-windowed dining-room. At the farther end was a mirror in a gilt frame. The other walls were full to overcrowding with portraits and conversation-pieces, but the room, with its white, fluted mantelpiece and its glistening table, had an air of ease and sedateness, as though, Sturgess said, "it expected you to sit over your wine." His host was pleased by that.

"That's the illusion we try to preserve," he said. "Not that we sit much, except to fill in forms. One has to choose in England nowadays: either to abandon the amenities altogether, put away everything that needs looking after — silver, china, good furniture — and drop down to the utility level; or to do nine-tenths of your own care and maintenance and, if you do it fast and efficiently enough, take your reward in a civilized evening now and then. We have, quite deliberately, chosen to work for what amenities are still possible. Tucker and Mrs.

Tucker are good old things, but they are slow and have no head. Marie makes up for that. She does half the housework herself and more than half of my form-filling, and still finds time to be intelligent. . . . But gradually, you know, things vanish into store. In spite of yourself, you cut down little by little. We shall have to do another clearance some day, I suppose — even pictures. I hate it, but it makes sense. Those chaps " — he indicated the portraits as he put down his empty glass — " had elbow-room in my people's old home. Here they ought rightly to take turns. Except, God knows, who am I to shut up any of them in a box-room ? "

The table, with two candelabra, was already set for dinner. Five places, Sturgess noticed, and his mind went back to the time when there had been five in the old granary at Pierre Chassaigne's.

How good it would be, he thought, if nothing had gone wrong and all of us were dining here this evening : Julian at the head of the table, Marie at the other end with her back to the mirror, I on her left, Frewer perhaps next to me, and opposite us, Heron, facing the window ! They would dine by daylight, the candelabra were no more than a decoration. The evening would come in on Heron's face, a tranquil, steadfast, unassailable face, and on his long hands, which he had a way of holding out before him, palms inward at the width of his body, as his talk became animated. He saw in imagination Heron rise from table when Marie rose and pass down the room to open the door for her, moving with long-striding grace and a carriage of his head, a slight indrawing of his chin, which gave ease to his erectness and yet tempted you to smile at it, so oddly did it resemble the drawing-back and curving-over of some superb question-mark or of a heron or of a knight in chess.

Sturgess couldn't recall how Lang had first come by the nickname, Heron, and had turned to ask Julian before he remembered that Julian had been a latecomer to the party at Blaise, and that either Frewer or he himself had invented the name, probably at the beginning of their journey, in the earliest days at Brussels.

But he had raised his head and encountered Julian's inquiring eyes.

"What were you gazing at?"

"Five?" Sturgess said, thinking that Julian must follow the train of his thought; but the blue eyes were, or seemed to be, still puzzled.

"'Five'? . . . Oh, I see. . . . We were to have had two other guests this evening: Mrs. Muriven — she's a neighbour, a friend of my mother's in the last two or three years before Mother died — and a girl she has staying with her. But it has been put off to to-morrow. Tucker is a bit slow, as you'll find. Having laid for five, five it remains. . . . You know," Julian continued as they left the dining-room and went upstairs together, "Tucker's mind interests me. It isn't just slow. It is incapable of drawing inferences. Unless someone says to him: 'You will have to take away those two places', he will let them stay there until we are actually sitting down to dinner and then begin to tut-tut and shake his head as if it were entangled in cobwebs. . . . But give him precise instructions very slowly, let him repeat them even more slowly, and he'll carry them out."

Sturgess's own imagination had been so powerfully seized by the idea he had expressed in the one word: "Five", that he found it hard to believe that Julian had not shared it. This casual talk about Tucker seemed at first an avoidance, but he found no hint of embarrassment in his host's manner. Perhaps I'm completely wrong, he said to himself. I suppose I have become obsessed by the subject or I shouldn't have had so clear a picture of Heron stalking about that dining-room. For weeks now I have been nursing the memory of the past and wanting the chance to talk of it with these two; but they, I dare say, have grown out of it; for them, it was an incident among a dozen others, and now they have other things to think about — their farm, their marriage, even Tucker's peculiarities.

"Here's your room," Julian said. He paused in mid-floor, looking carefully round to see that his guest had all he might need.

"It's a charming room," Sturgess said, and he began to pay compliments to the house, feeling as he did so that his politeness and Julian's casual talk, each in its own way, contradicted his expectation of their re-encounter. It was as if there were not, and had never been, an exceptional link between them. It's as if I'd come to the wrong play, he thought. But that's absurd, he added. Indefinable barriers often grow up between people for no good reason except that some foolish shyness prevents them from speaking the direct word that each wants to speak; and, as he took out his keys and began to unlock a suitcase, he said: "Tell me more of Marie. How is she? I hope she's well?"

It was a question that he ought to have asked, and that Julian, by some explanation of his wife's absence, ought to have answered, long ago. But Julian seemed to be unaware of this, and spoke of her easily, too easily, as though he had really forgotten that his guest had not set eyes on Marie since that night in France four years ago. She was well, he said. England seemed to suit her, though she found Mrs. Tucker a stubborn pupil as a cook. She had gone into Tarryford to see Mrs. Muriven.

With this, Julian retreated towards the door. "Well," he said, "I'll leave you to settle in. When you're ready there'll be tea downstairs. You will find Marie there. She'll blame herself for not having been here when you came."

4

Left alone by his host, Sturgess unlocked two of his suitcases, and took out the gifts he had brought from New York. What queer gifts one brought to England nowadays: sugar, plain chocolate, cans of butter. He laid them out on the floor, hoping he had chosen rightly, but troubled in his heart because what he had brought was so undecorative, so unashamedly useful. There were, however, two bottles, one of perfume, the other of old cognac, for Marie, because she was French. She was not, as he remembered her, a girl who smiled readily, but sometimes her upper lip curved and her small teeth smiled for her; she would, he hoped, smile in this way when she received his gift.

Instead of unpacking as he had intended, he went to one of the two windows of his bedroom and looked down at the Gloucestershire landscape, only to find that he wasn't taking it in. He was staring at it, but seeing nothing except that it was green and pleasant and almost disconcertingly peaceful.

His mind was in the past again. That he had lived through those days in the upper room of Marie Chassaigne's house, and through one night in particular; that he had used his intelligence and played his part in what was then done, both shocked and pleased him. It pleased him the more because it was exceptional to the life he had formerly led, and to the life he would lead in future. He had been brought up, at his mother's home in Maine, to think of war not only with abhorrence but almost with contempt. Such was his theory still. And yet he had learned by his experience; it had revealed to him an intensity, a peril, in the act of living that he would not otherwise have guessed at. In his early years, certain things — for example, that men wouldn't turn into stampeding herds — had been too easily taken for granted. It had been assumed that, when difficulties arose, you discussed them reasonably, compromised, or in extreme cases went to law. Of course there were foreign wars, and probably would be again, but these were to be thought of, if thought of at all, in terms of remote battlefields. They didn't come into private houses — at any rate not into your own house — and convert ordinary domestic life into an insanity of subterfuge, of lying and hiding, of being prepared without hesitation or discussion to kill.

Now he knew — perhaps he had always known, but now he felt — that wars did precisely this, and that, in doing so, they gave a new edge to all experience, not to warlike experience only; they gave a new edge to the life of peace and to the peaceable appearances of mankind, so that nothing was to be taken for granted. His home in Maine, and every tree that grew there, and the great log-fire in winter, and his books, were miraculous because no one was in hiding, no one pursued, no one on the point of death. His students presented to him a new appearance of exceptional good fortune (and perhaps, also, of missing something) because their youth was sheltered, because they were neither invaders nor the invaded, and belonged to no underground movement, and had an even continuity in their lives.

He slid up the lower sash of the window and leaned out. Why was he uneasy? All was well with him at home, and here, at this instant, there was just enough breeze to give the air a delicious coolness. Downstairs, in this small, graceful house, were the two friends whom he had come so far to see. Tea was probably ready by now and Marie waiting. They were expecting him to appear. Why did he hesitate?

Having little patience with any introspective mood in himself that tied him down, he came away from the window with a quick decisive step. The rest of his unpacking could wait. He would take a few of his gifts as an introduction to Marie and go downstairs at once.

He lodged the two bottles, the perfume and the cognac, in the crook of his arm, and went out on to the landing. Voices came up from the hall: Marie's unmistakably, with that evenness of stress and absence of any drawling syllable which were the only trace of French intonation in her speaking English; and another feminine voice, lower in pitch, stronger and yet quieter in tone, with a vibrant quality of deep strings. This stranger's voice, with evocative power of a kind belonging more often to a scent than to a sound, produced in Sturgess a momentary impression that, as well as hearing, he was remembering it; but what, for an instant, had appeared to be memory did not crystallize in any image of the past, the seeming echo declared no origin, and he scouted it as a flagrant example of romantic self-deception. With his hand on the banister, he smiled at himself the corrective smile of common sense. It wasn't the first time he had been fooled; he had been entranced before by women's voices and ridiculously disillusioned by later appearances. Nevertheless he stood still, hoping she would speak again.

"You will no doubt think it strange," Marie was saying with the formality of phrase which, when she was not perfectly at ease, reminded one that she had been a teacher of English, "that I of all people should press a German book on you, but truly, as you read German and already know Goethe so well, I can't let you go away without *Elective Affinities*. A good novel, it is *not*; it is clumsy and awkward; he tries to say too much all at once; but just for that reason. . . ."

They must have come to the front door; Marie was facing outwards and he did not hear her last words; but he heard the girl make some answer that deprecated this gap in her own reading and paid tribute to the French thoroughness.

"But I am by no means a German scholar," Marie said.

"Nor am I, I promise you. I'm not a scholar at all. It just happens to be a natural language with me. I had a German grandmother who brought me up on it."

They were on the porch now, saying good-bye.

"Well," the girl said, "I look forward to to-morrow evening. We shall be able to talk about it then."

Marie laughed. "You must be a fast reader!"

"I don't know about that," the other replied, laughing too — deep, leisurely laughter which called up into Sturgess's mind an image of her face and body as though she had been visible to him. "But I shall have read *some* of it."

"*Some* of it" — how her voice dwelt on the word! Sturgess shrugged his shoulders and readjusted the two bottles he was carrying. There are women who talk like that in the deep South, he thought. I suppose that is all . . . But, as he went downstairs, the syllable was thrilling in him, as though it were across his strings that the bow had been drawn.

5

Marie's greeting had none of the easy, or the studied, casualness of Julian's. If she too had behaved as though the past were shut out of her mind, Sturgess could not have endured it. She was, for him, quite simply, a heroine. The long service she had done in the River Line, the long suffering at Ravensbrück, might have been title enough, but not these alone, or even these chiefly, gave her title in his mind. He had seen her take a decision and give effect to it in a way that had changed his whole conception of the power and the nature of women. She had become, for him, legendary, and when, returning from the front door, her back to the light, she saw him and quickened her step and stretched out both her hands with a little cry of welcome, he tried to express his feeling by taking her right hand only and kissing it. The impulse was spontaneous, but the action, being against his custom, checked him; when he looked up none of the words of greeting would come. He saw tears in her eyes and could say nothing.

But never for more than an instant did Marie lose command of herself.

"Come!" she said, turning back across the hall towards the room that faced the dining-room. "Dear Philip. . . . I'm glad, I'm glad. . . . There!" She tossed her head and made herself laugh. "How can I take your arm if you carry — what are you carrying? Bottles?"

Julian, by an opposite door, came into the little drawing-room as they entered it. The giving of presents and the pouring out of tea released their tongues, and Sturgess felt his mood change. As though he had been afraid and the reason for his fear had been removed, he was suddenly as happy as a shy boy who finds at a party that he is a success. He leaned back firmly in his chair — he had been nervously sitting too far forward in it — and settled down to talk, to listen eagerly, to observe his surroundings with ever-increasing pleasure: the Sheraton cabinets gleaming with porcelain that he couldn't yet distinguish, the Battersea flute-players and shepherdesses on the mantelpiece, the scrolled flowers of the carpet at his feet, the Rockingham cup and saucer in his hands. While they talked, his eyes moved approvingly over the beautiful, mixed furniture with its upholstery of green and rosy stripes, faded and shredded.

The blaze of full afternoon having gone, a deepening sunlight looked in with the calm of a long familiar visitor, slowly moving its sparkle across the panes of the Sheraton and sliding its gold along the shelves and into a shell-recess beyond. That Tucker was responsible for the upkeep of this room was so evidently impossible that Sturgess was tempted to compliment Marie on her care of it, but he refrained, guessing that her pleasure was to forget housework when it was done, not to be praised for it.

"And what, may I ask, are you doing in England?" Julian inquired.

"Visiting you."

"Nothing else? You generally have a solemn purpose, Philip, as well as a frivolous one!"

His special form of banter, a pretended paternalism towards Sturgess's supposed boyishness, was answered with a grin. Sturgess liked it without being in the least deceived by it, knowing well enough that it was Julian's method, partly ironical and partly affectionate, of tempting him to give himself away. " You know, Marie," Julian now exclaimed, " we are entertaining an extremely odd animal! On the surface, as simple as can be — much too simple to be true."

" By which you mean ? " said Sturgess.

" On the surface, practical, cheerful, not introspective, not self-conscious, all the virtues of a good citizen and a good mixer, clear as glass, sound as a bell, healthy and happy — all the clichés that we are taught as schoolboys to venerate. Not a whiff of metaphysics anywhere. . . . But below the surface — what ? I suspect a subtle Puritan ancestor. And behind that——" He broke off and laughed. " True, Philip ? "

" A grain of truth."

Julian took a pipe from his pocket and rubbed its bowl on his knee. " At Blaise, I remember, you had a long discussion on the nature of being."

" Why not ? " Marie intervened. " Why are you laughing at him ? It's a very interesting subject."

Julian smiled. " Indeed I'm not laughing. I was another part of that discussion. Of course it's interesting to you, Marie, but as an intellectual exercise ; your mind, bless you, works that way. But Philip is interested from — from another point of view ? . . . True ? "

" A grain," Sturgess acknowledged. " Probably I talked nonsense."

" There you are ! " Julian exclaimed. " Listen to him ! 'Probably I talked nonsense !' Never have I met a man who put up such a wall of the practical, the cheerful, the unintrospective — all the rest of it — between——"

" Training, perhaps," said Sturgess, " or environment. I don't know. . . . I try not to talk bigger than I am.

Sometimes I do. I expect I did in that discussion at Blaise. Probably out of my depth."

"One of the ways of learning to swim," Julian rejoined: then faster and with quiet, bitter energy: "Life doesn't consist in standing on the beach and selling peanuts in paper bags. Better swim. Better drown if necessary. Come out on the other side." It was said with so sharp a spurt of vehemence that Julian himself was surprised by it and, with a little gesture of impatience, waved it away. "Well," he said, "now it is I who am talking!"

Odd, Sturgess thought, Julian doesn't often give you even a glimpse through his defences; and in a companionable wish to make things easy he said: "That, in a way, brings us back to the question you first asked: what am I doing here?"

Julian recovered his irony; his eyebrows went up. "Investigating the nature of being? Wonderful! Are you preparing a thesis?"

"No," Sturgess answered, now stubbornly but good-humouredly determined not to be talked down. "And we needn't give the thing quite so grandiose a name as the 'nature of being'. But the world is in an unspeakable mess. Everyone talks of 'frustration', which means what? — that whichever way you turn, left or right, you are up against it. No way out that anyone can see. All the expedients built on the idea that man is a political animal or an economic animal appear to have been exhausted; U.N.O. began to rot as soon as it was born. And I thought — not because I proposed to convert the world, but because I wanted to find a way to live — I thought it would be worth while to ask again what the human personality is. Not intellectual exercise. A practical question, God knows. If it isn't a fragment of Class and it isn't a fragment of Nation— You see," he said, looking from one to the other with embarrassment and wishing he hadn't gone so far, " what is now called ' frustration ' looks to me very like what used to be called ' tragedy ' about twenty-three centuries ago. Man thinking he's in a trap, and in it because he thinks he is. And on this level — the level, I mean, on which rival ideologies are for ever wanting our bodies to change their uniforms — I think he is in a trap. It has all the grip and finality of tragedy. And if he exists only on this level, as the materialists say, then that's the end. And even if there's another world, that doesn't help us here if we are cut off from it. But if the human personality doesn't have its being on this level only, but exists in depth — here and now three-dimensional, not two — then there's a way of living in depth."

Julian answered: " As you say: ' a practical question, God knows,' " but Marie put in:

" Does tragedy teach that ? "

" Doesn't it ? Tragedy isn't a shut box. If it were——"

" *Athalie ?* "

" Marie, you know I can't debate Racine with you."

" *Lear* then ? Did he find ' a way of living in depth ' ? "

" I think he did."

" He went mad."

" And sane."

She did not answer. They were, he knew, far apart.

" Well," said Julian, stretching his legs out before him and using the cautiously casual tone of an elder to a younger brother, " well, there it is after all. You have come three thousand miles to take soundings in the human personality. Good. But why Europe ? "

It was a question to which Sturgess was altogether

unprepared to give a straight answer. Blaise was a part of the answer, and Heron a part. All he found to say was:

" Only a notion that, if ever I found a hint of what I am after, I might find it here."

" In Europe? In England?"

" In this house." As that explanation was inadequate, even to himself, he stumbled on: " During that discussion at Blaise, on this subject more or less, Heron said——"

He stopped there in obedience to a little exclamation which made him think that Julian intended to interrupt, but Julian after all said nothing, and Sturgess did not continue.

When tea was over, they took him through the house, first into the den, from which Julian had come into the drawing-room, and which had long windows opening into the garden; then, across the hall and through the dining-room, into a corresponding room that was heavy with the scent of old leather bindings; and afterwards upstairs to their own bedroom and a small central room with a balcony above the porch which, Marie said, was her own. There were two bowls of white roses, and a giant vase of long sprays, tipped with starry pink, whose name Sturgess did not know. To his eye, it was, in all other respects, a curiously unfeminine room which she seemed to have taken over with her husband.

On the walls chiefly etchings, on the furniture old leather.

" Mostly overflow from the library at Tarryford," she explained, " but that — you remember that?"

It was a blue river-scene of Sisley's that had hung in her father's room at Blaise, and Sturgess remembered it well.

" It surprised me that the Germans didn't take it," he said now, " but Heron said they never would, because your father was a poet and they didn't want the reputation of barbarians."

" And look at this, Philip," Julian intervened abruptly from the opposite wall of the room, standing aside from a drawing in ink and wash that hung there. " According to my grandfather's tradition it's Gainsborough. Rather formal. Very early, my grandfather said. I like the flicker of those bunchy trees."

But Sturgess was slow to be diverted. His eyes were on the Sisley. " And I suppose," he said, " that, on the psychology of Germans, Heron could at any rate claim to be an authority."

As he said this, he turned, without suspicion of harm, to look at the Gainsborough, and found Julian gazing at Marie with watchful anxiety. There was an instant's silence; but it was not the silence, it was the speed with which Marie covered it, that gave Sturgess a sense of having been maladroit.

" Yes," she said, " you are right."

He knew that for a moment — it was always a sign of disturbance in her — she was thinking in French and unconsciously translating: *Oui, vous avez raison.* Then she continued: " In any case, my father loved that picture. To have buried it in a cellar would have been for him a kind of sacrilege — or surrender. How right he was! Even when I was arrested, they spared his life and spared his picture. Why? Because they respect artists? Because they are intellectual snobs? Who shall say?" Permitting no further word of Heron, she pushed up the window's lower sash as far as it would go, and, stooping, went out on to the balcony.

" Look," she said, " it's lovely here. We might have our coffee here this evening and your cognac, Philip. Or shall it be on the lawn?"

The little stress, if it had been a stress, was ended. They stayed on the balcony for almost an hour, then began to separate to bath and change. Julian set out for the cellar.

"To-morrow we shall be five and a little cautious. But to-night is a private celebration." He lifted his hand towards his wife with a movement of protective tenderness which Sturgess found the more charming because it stopped short within an inch of touching her. "Take warning, Philip. Never marry a Frenchwoman. They have a taste in wine. Even your cellar isn't your own. . . . What shall it be, Marie, the Chambertin or the Latour?"

"Am I to choose? Then, the Musigny. It's too warm a night for the Chambertin, and, though you may not believe it, Julian, that Latour will improve yet, if you leave it alone."

Julian laughed aloud and flourished a long hand as he went downstairs. "What did I tell you? She is my Saintsbury and my Simon too! Will that do as blank verse?"

Well, Sturgess thought as he closed the door of his own room, at any rate they are very much in love. But whether they are altogether at ease, I wonder.

6

WHEN he was dressed, he found Marie on the porch, and sat there with her, waiting for Julian to come down. Her suffering had not dulled her appearance but made it brittle, as though she were living always in that condition of energy which comes to men on the second flood of sleeplessness, when they have passed beyond the relaxation of being consciously tired. She said abruptly, as though she had been waiting to say it and was determined to have it said before they were interrupted :

" Philip, I want to ask you something quite frankly. Do you intend to write about what happened at Blaise ? "

" Why, Marie ? What makes you ask that ? "

" After you came back to England and before you were transferred to Washington, you saw Julian now and then. He says you spoke of writing. He says you spoke of it the last time he saw you, just before you left for America, a few weeks before the Normandy landing. He says it was very much in your mind. Have you in fact written ? "

" Not *written*. I have made notes. Making notes is a bad habit of mine."

To his surprise, she said seriously: " It is a bad habit."

" But why ? "

" People read them in the end." She jerked her head and sighed. " Oh, I suppose secrecy, too, is a habit that grows on one ! Julian also has it. You aren't dropped into France as an agent without learning to keep your mouth shut and to hate the sight of anything in your own handwriting. I have exactly the same feeling. . . . If you write, do you propose to publish ? "

" I suppose so, Marie, in the end. An old man's memoirs some day. Not the River Line only, though that, in a special way, means a lot to me. I was pretty raw, you know. In America, when you're young, life seems made for you. Even if you happen to be poor and it doesn't look that way at first, you believe that it will; you're taught that it will or anyhow that it ought to. Life isn't hostile, that's the point; it's something to discover and take from and enjoy, not something to endure and defend yourself against. And at long last the American view is the sane one, or so I believe. But I learnt at Blaise to understand Thomas Hardy better than I did."

" Hardy ? "

" ' The President of the Immortals . . . had ended his sport with Tess. . . .' "

There was a little pause. " Isn't it strange ? " she said. " We are both teachers of English, and I am sick of that quotation. It seems so small a part of Hardy to me. But I suppose that, in neither of our two countries, is he much loved or really understood. I wonder what Julian would say." She had been speaking meditatively, but the occurrence of Julian's name quickened her tone as though it had reminded her that he was likely to interrupt them, and she added with irony: " Could you not — how shall I say it ? — could you not distil your experience in a monograph on Hardy without mentioning Blaise ? "

Whether to take this seriously or not he scarcely knew, and while he hesitated she said to his surprise: " For Father's sake, I should like an account to be written, for publication perhaps when we are all dead, but if you publish now or at any time in the foreseeable future, you must change not only the names of the people and the places, you must change character and scenery, you must say nothing — not one word or hint — that would enable the River Line to be traced."

He did not dispute it. On this subject now, as in the past, he took her orders, and he pledged himself at once that it should be as she wished. "But still, Marie," he said, "I don't understand. It's all over. The Germans are out of France. What harm can the names do now?"

"Ah," she said, "the Rhine is not as broad as the Atlantic. Nor is the Oder. . . . There are always enemies of France in the world, and of England — and of America too, O thou of too much faith! Why should we tell them anything? The Japanese are out of the Philippines, but you will be sorry some day — or your grandchildren will be sorry — that you have let out so many secrets since the war ended. Be silent, be silent, be silent until Armageddon is over. It is by no means over yet. They captured me; they captured two others; but even now they couldn't begin to chart a map of the River Line."

"'They'?" he interrupted. "The Nazis? They are dead or in prison."

"'Nazi'," she answered, "has become a self-deceiving word. The Germans do not die; they are too vigorous a nation. The herd-peoples are still moving westward. Twice the flood has been thrown back. There is a third to come. The extreme Right and the extreme Left, the men of blood who, under different names, are entered into the same conspiracy against us, do not die. They wait their time. Don't help them, my friend. If you must publish, conceal names, disguise places. Father's reputation will wait."

"Reputation? As a man of letters?"

She shook her head. " I mean — as a Frenchman. . . . As a poet, he wasn't greatly famous except among a few, but that will come ; in the end he will have his place in our literature, not a giant's place but a lasting one I think. I'm not troubled on that score. But as a Frenchman . . . You see, Philip, Father, who had an almost insane hatred of Germans, didn't give that impression to the ordinary citizens of Blaise. Because I insisted that he should, he even received Germans in our house to give cover to me. Ordinary people knew nothing of his reasons ; they trusted me personally, but they didn't even know that the River Line existed ; and naturally, when I was taken and Father was spared, they assumed that he had been at least complaisant. He died so soon after the liberation — I didn't see him again — that the cloud lingers. Your book would disperse it. Nevertheless, your book must wait. . . . Besides," she said unguardedly, " if you wrote it now, you would write it wrong."

He was quick to ask : in what way ? " I know," he said modestly, " there's much you can tell me that would clear up doubts in my mind. But why should my account be wrong in any essentials ? "

She put up her guard again — or so he thought — and deliberately eluded him. " I was speaking," she answered, " of my father. You scarcely knew him," and she spoke of Chassaigne with so much feeling, so characteristic a mingling of irony and affection, that Sturgess was almost ashamed of his knowledge that she was eluding him.

" You know," she said, looking into his eyes as if she doubted whether he would understand what she now wished to say, " the noblest part of it was that he, to whom independence was the very salt of life and whose obedient daughter I had always been, took orders from me. Blindly, without question. Once, he almost rebelled.

After that, never. He made his act of acceptance and stood by it. I had told him — never mind why; there was good reason — that he must stay indoors all day. 'Why?' he said. 'We have no English visitors in the granary. It is spring. Why must I be cooped up like a hen? Give me an intelligible reason.' I had none that I might give, even to him. I said so, and his face darkened. I thought he was going to refuse. Then, with a patient shrug, he reached for a pen, dipped it, and said: 'Very well, the word Why is abolished. *Le mot Pourquoi est aboli. . . .* After all it is not, as some materialists have supposed, the most precious word in the French language.' I asked him: 'Which is the most precious word?' He answered with a smile that it was the word Who, used interrogatively. That emphasis on the mystery of personality, which I have never been able . . . fully . . . to share, was the key to Father's thought," Marie said, and she repeated: "'*Le mot le plus précieux de notre langue? Eh bien, mon enfant, c'est le mot Qui, employé interrogativement. Là réside le génie de Pascal et même de Montaigne. C'est vraiment le génie de la France.*'"

She had begun this small reminiscence, Sturgess knew, to divert his question; she ended it with passion, her love for her father, and her own sceptical mind, speaking in it. Julian, coming out on to the porch with a decanter of sherry, heard the final words. As he offered her a glass and she refused it with an inclination of her hand that was scarcely a gesture, he let his eyes rest on her face, then turned away. On what dangerous ground had she been treading? his eyes had seemed to ask, and he looked back to her again with anxiety and tenderness. But experience had taught her only too well not to cry. The quality of her body in repose was that of a steel spring; she moved with the grace of a small tigress; no one, Sturgess supposed, had ever believed that she could tire unless they had seen her, as he had done now and then in the granary at Blaise, with the lids down over her unfierce, indomitable eyes. She shut them now for an instant and was still, a pulse in her throat vibrating; then reached out to the decanter on the stone balustrade and shut her fingers round its neck. The white of her finger-joints and the narrow brown forearm tautened by that grip, Sturgess wouldn't forget, nor her return to the discreet commonplace.

"It is time to eat," she said. "I will go to see how Mrs. Tucker is getting on."

7

DURING that evening and the following day, it was borne in upon Sturgess that, though each of his hosts could be persuaded without difficulty to talk of Blaise when alone with him, each avoided the subject — or at any rate what he regarded as the vital part of it — in the other's presence. Then they swerved instantly, as they had when he was looking at Sisley's landscape, from any word of Heron; and though, separately, they would let him say his say and listen to him politely, he felt that he was trespassing.

Julian even went so far as to offer an explanation: that he was always careful with Marie on the subject of Blaise because the thought of her father's death was painful to her. Sturgess nodded with good-humoured understanding, but the explanation seemed to him by no means plausible. Pierre Chassaigne had been dead almost three years; Marie wasn't of a kind to wrap up the memory of him in a gloomy silence; what was more, she herself had deliberately spoken of him, recalling his appearance, his words, his behaviour, with loving frankness. Oh, no, Sturgess thought, old Chassaigne isn't the subject they are avoiding!

The avoidance troubled him because the reason for it, which he saw clearly enough, threatened the marriage of his friends. If they dared not speak of Heron because Marie had loved him, they were allowing the recollection of him to be a barrier between them — a barrier which would not vanish because they pretended that it was not there, but would grow. Sturgess had no doubt that it was wrong in psychological theory, and vain in practice, to muffle the past with cautious silences; you must bring it to the surface, give it light, talk freely of it, recognize it; then it would cease to have power over you. Marie and Julian were evidently far from understanding this, and Sturgess didn't see how he could, within the rules of courtesy, enlighten them. If they had been American, it would have been easier, but the French and the English, in matters of personal psychology, were stubbornly old-fashioned. Tell them they were " cases ", and instead of being interested they went right back into their shells.

And Sturgess had no wish to drive Marie and Julian into their shells. Blind they might be, but, in their own way, they were happy, and certainly good company. He spent all the morning on the farm with Julian and a great part of the afternoon helping Marie find her way through the entanglement of paper-work that fell to her. The steadiness, the competence and the good-humour with which they did their work impressed him. He was delighted to be used, to be assigned tasks and given orders at one moment and to be consulted about American methods in the next. It was like being taken into a partnership that renewed the partnership of Blaise. And when the day was done, it was done. They knew not only how to work but how to stop. Julian came in, Marie glanced at him, closed her books and put them away.

" I am going to the kitchen before I go to my bath. When I come out, everything that can be done will have been done. After that, I shall be a lady of leisure, though the heavens fall. This is going to be a civilized evening. I like our guests — all three."

" Mrs. Muriven can be good value," Julian answered.

" My mother called her the Iron Duke, which doesn't prevent her from being as feminine as anyone I know."

" I liked the girl too," Marie said. " English girls of character take time to know, but I'd trust this one in a tight corner."

At this Sturgess opened his eyes. " That from you, Marie, is something ! "

" From me ? "

" You are a judge of tight corners."

She shrugged her shoulders. " But am I of English women ? . . . You didn't see her, Philip."

" No, but I heard her."

" Heard ? "

" Her voice — in the hall, talking to you about Goethe."

Marie paused as if she were listening. " Yes," she said, " now you speak of it — it is a memorable voice."

8

Sturgess, who could bath and dress faster than most men on earth, came down to the drawing-room before his hosts. He was careful for his appearance, particularly on that evening when guests were expected, and, knowing that the tying of bow-ties was not among his natural gifts, examined himself in the looking-glass over the mantelpiece. It was old, its glass backed by tin amalgam, and gave to the image of his head and of the windows behind him the mellow clearness of portraiture darkened by time. His sudden thought was that it made him look more "like himself" than looking-glasses commonly did, and when he had made sure that his tie was straight and had noticed how whitely the wings of his collar gleamed against the throat browned by his voyage, he paused to examine the boy who looked out at him from the face of the man, and to remember the snub-nose now straightened, the cheeks thin then in an indeterminate way but now bonily set, and the short, leaping, surprised hair which, though now disciplined, had still a look of inquiry. Presentable, he thought with a grin, but, as my blessed mother says, still a bit guileless.

He turned to watch Tucker laboriously entering with a silver tray heavy with bottles, glasses and ice. At sight of the American gentleman, the little man's face brightened into a round hospitable grin. As he put down the tray, he looked over his shoulder as mincingly as a girl who hopes that someone will notice the new dress she is wearing; then, standing out of the way so that his treasure might be seen, rolled his head in expectation of applause. Sturgess, though willing, was uncertain. What should he applaud? Scarcely the bottles, though gin was rare. The tray, perhaps — but the polishing of it he suspected of being Marie's, or even Julian's, work. Then his eye fell upon the ice-bucket and he remembered that in England, above all in the country, ice was by no means to be taken for granted.

"Ice!" he said in the appropriate tone of astonishment.

Tucker fell into a flutter of pride. "Of course now, in America ice wouldn't be nothing out of the ordinary, I know. But this we had to bring ourselves from Kemble, wrapped in a blanket. . . . And Madam said," he continued with the emphasis of a Moses descended from Sinai, "she said you was please to mix the cocktails before she came down." He began to clasp and unclasp his hands. "For *seven*, Madam said."

Sturgess willingly obeyed; two brimming glasses were carried off to the kitchen; and he seated himself in a chair by the window at peace with the world, consciously and happily tranquil, to await his hosts' coming. They came in together and sat with him. It was the first time he had seen Marie in an evening frock.

"And it may be the last," she said with a smile. "Occasions are rare."

"Still, it's good to see you. Don't forget that I'm a new-boy. I haven't seen you since the war was won."

She looked at him. "Yes, it was won, wasn't it?" Then at Julian: "Philip is right. What has happened since, and what may happen, is no reason for not being happy in the simple fact. Those who believed in 1940 that the Germans had already won were wrong. That is something after all."

"From my point of view," Julian answered, "a strictly professional one, Philip, I grant you — it's enough to be going on with. Utopia never was my promised land, so I'm not easily disappointed. . . . I think I hear our guests. How odd! Marie in a party frock. Guests coming. Me — here! I was a boy in this house."

Tucker, to whom the reporting of news was an irresistible delight, put his head in through the door to say that he thought the ladies was coming now, as indeed they audibly were, Mrs. Muriven's Ford being a veteran. There was a pause, and the sound of Tucker's slow, welcoming conversation. The door opened again; he announced the guests in tones of warm approval, then lingered to gaze, his smile and his eyes dwelling upon the younger of the two ladies as though he were a conjuror who had wonderfully produced her out of a hat.

"But we have already met," Mrs. Muriven said. "Valerie, this is the kind American I met in the train."

The appearance of the girl who gave him her hand so accorded with her voice already heard that the harmony at once delighted and astonished him. He was aware, too, or partly aware, of a further echo within her actual presence, and might have stayed too long, striving to identify it. He had to compel himself to release her hand, to take his eyes away from her face, and to speak, to her and Mrs. Muriven indifferently, the polite openings of conversation.

"You are in command," Marie said with a glance towards the silver tray, and, when he had poured out drinks and Julian had taken them from him, he watched the girl move forward half a pace to receive hers, and thought of a sapling moved by the wind and straightening itself again. The impression that her grace made upon him had in it so much of the quality of memory that he seemed against reason to be looking back upon this instant's freshness. This is the first time I have seen her, the first time I have touched her! he said to himself, hardly believing it. The thought that all the hours of that evening lay before him filled him with the extravagance of riches yet to be spent, and his fingers tightened on the icy bowl of his glass.

" My godmother tells me that even in the train you were smiling to yourself," she said, the flicker of an upward curve appearing in each corner of her mouth.

He hesitated a moment, listening to the after-tone of her voice. " I expect I was. I had a friend once who told me that I had the habit of grinning, even when the Germans were on our tracks. I like arriving places. I expect I was smiling at the thought of the good days ahead."

" Are they always ' good days ' ? "

" In a way, yes. . . . These are certainly." Then he heard himself add : " I think this is the most beautiful room I have ever been in," and, to give cover to that wild irrelevance, he turned, an instant too late, from her to the room. Too late, for he had seen her lips part for the intake of sudden breath, and, when he looked at her again, there was new colour in her cheeks.

" These days are among the last I shall spend in England," she said. " I am waiting for my passage. It may come through at any time now."

" Passage ? " he exclaimed. " To the United States ? "

His eagerness was so unguarded that her eyes shone with laughter. The modesty of her laughing in the way she did, discounting his seriousness ; the good grace of her taking for granted his willingness to be laughed at, enchanted him. " No," she answered, " South Africa. I have a married brother there. I am going to live with him."

No doubt this was true, but none of it did he believe. All his years were being gathered into this moment; his whole being was concentrated in it; he was released to an enraptured confidence in which South Africa had no place.

She turned away to put down her empty glass. As her body swung and her arm stretched down to a table at knee-level, how she held up her head!

9

THOUGH, in the dining-room, where shafts of sunlight renewed the pictures' gilding, his conversation was at first with Mrs. Muriven on his left — in Frewer's seat, he thought — his eyes moved often across the table that he might witness and remember that evening's window-light on Valerie Barton's face.

He watched her with discretion but with rare intensity — intensity of a specially selective kind ; not generalizing, not so much admiring her beauty or observing the character of her face as marking the points of vitality — the glint of a lip moving, the starting up of a cluster of hair that she had pressed back from her temple, the glow and the little tensions of her flesh as the head turned — the fact, and the piercing, miraculous evidences of the fact, that she was alive.

Why miraculous ? Not because he was a sentimental fool who had fallen in love with a girl he didn't know. That might be ; but this was independent of it. The edge of happiness as of suffering, the keenness of experience itself, is often in the reflection that it might not have been ; that we might not have opened fortune's book at the particular page which now lies before us, exhibiting miraculously, in the light of our day, lyric or elegy that we did not know we had written ; the book might have opened at another page or this page have been blank. The chair on which she sat might have been empty and his view of the fluted mantelpiece uninterrupted. He might have been staring now at the exposed back of her chair and thinking that this was Heron's place, as he had thought that Mrs. Muriven was in Frewer's. Instead, instead of nothingness, she was there, and alive; a white reflection on the table moved under her wrist; and, the table being small, he could — now, if he chose, but he didn't choose — break into her conversation with Marie, and see her eyes come round to his and hear her voice speak to him.

Having the power to work this miracle, he did not choose as yet to exercise it. He was determined to keep his head, and joined peacefully in Julian's and Mrs. Muriven's talk, which at the moment was of agriculture with an admixture of politics. But interest flowed easily at that table; conversation did not settle into compartments, but embraced now two, now three, now five; and he, given an opportunity by a question of Marie's, soon found himself chattering to Valerie about everything on earth from the music of Delius to the character of George Washington and the pleasure of sea voyages. Her voyage to South Africa, she said, wouldn't be long enough for her. She would like to go round the world in a sailing-ship — no newspaper, no wireless; a little " plain company " and all the books she wanted to read again.

" Again ? " he said. " No new books ? "

" Oh, yes, those as well."

" Which old books in particular ? "

" That would be a confessional catalogue ! "

" And what on earth did you mean by ' plain company ' ? "

" People getting on with their own jobs: makers or healers or endurers: not agitators. Seamen, merchants, doctors, soldiers — does that seem dull ? "

" Not if it includes schoolmasters."

" By no means all ! "

" One," he said, " would be enough. Where can I find a sailing-ship ? "

It was pleasant to fool with her and to let the minutes slide by, not caring, sure for once they couldn't be better spent.

" You are in form," Marie said in a quiet aside.

" ' Let the world slip,' " he answered, " ' we shall ne'er be younger.' "

But before dinner was over, the world returned. Mrs. Muriven brought it back. He had been looking over the side of Valerie's sailing-ship, watching fantastic water rise and pass and fall away astern like the peaceful hours, and had been listening to Mrs. Muriven with half-attentive ear.

" No," she said, emerging from discussion with Julian, " I'm not at all sure that you are the right person for me to argue with."

" Because I agree too much ? " Julian replied.

" You act decisively enough ; I don't doubt it ; but only because, as a naval officer, you have been trained to it. Outside your job, you aren't interested in my revolutionary doctrine. You live by it yourself, but as for the world in general—" She turned from Julian in mock despair. " Mr. Sturgess will be more profitable to quarrel with."

" Mrs. Muriven," Julian explained, with a flicker of amusement, " believes that the Western democracies are dying of a sick-conscience which makes them hesitate to act at all and, if ever they do act, turns their action sour with self-criticism. Example, the Versailles Treaty. Example, Hiroshima. Example, the deadly paralysis of policy in Germany. She exempts me in practice, but only I'm afraid because she thinks my conscience has been anaesthetized. Does the charge strike home to you, Philip ? "

A sick-conscience ? . . . Sturgess had never supposed himself to possess one. It appeared to him as a refinement of intellectualism to which he didn't pretend. One could carry introspection too far; though he couldn't claim to be without the habit, he had always checked it in himself. A healthy and hopeful mind in a healthy body was what he aimed at — a naïve ambition, perhaps, but his own.

" No," he said, " I don't think it does strike home."

Suddenly it did, for Mrs. Muriven said: " At least Julian has been trained not to cry over spilt decisions."

Sturgess looked at her sharply. If she had known all that had happened at Blaise, she could not have uttered a more penetrating comment on his attitude towards his own share in those happenings. Wasn't he proud — almost struttingly proud — of having taken a drastic, a *military* decision; in his heart, he wanted Julian and Marie to applaud him for it. At the same time, he was appalled by the consequences of that decision: in his heart, he wanted his responsibility to be lifted from him. . . . My God, he said to himself, am I as infirm as that ? Is that really what I came to England for; to be patted on the back and to be comfortably absolved ? . . . The pang of this possibility was so sharp that his mind gave to Mrs. Muriven's saying a new form: at least Julian has been trained not to cry over spilt blood.

His remedy for this embarrassment of the soul was the plain one of telling himself not to be a self-conscious ass. His sane instinct was to turn his thought outward, to thank heaven for what good there was — friendship, the beauty of women, the summer's day; and to give his mind to cares other than his own. His reward was to find

Mrs. Muriven challenging, and, if you took her with a pinch of good American salt, valuable.

Where the democracies had failed or were failing, the epitaph, she declared, was always a double one: in the matter of taking, " Too much, too soon "; in the matter of paying, " Too little, too late."

" In America," she said, " you probably don't notice it as we do. You can afford the time-lag. I know what it feels like. I am a Victorian myself, and you, in America, are living in what we called Victorian security—"

At that he opened such sceptical eyes that she paused to meet them.

" But it's true in effect," she lightly insisted, " as true as historical comparisons ever are! You have so much that we had then — gigantic resources, a broad margin of error for boasts and blunders, an ever-increasing power, an ever-growing responsibility. You are becoming — though you will have to forgive the much-abused word — it is a word of service, not of seizure, as I understand it — you are becoming an imperial people." She threw up her head to provoke him. " You are approaching the Jubilee! "

He laughed aloud, delighted by her banter. " Not in manners! " he exclaimed. " Nor in morals perhaps? "

" Not in detail," she conceded, adapting her tone to his with a grace which told that she approved the young American who knew how to play not too solemnly her serious game. " Not in detail. . . . But in temperament? — I wonder! Your writers speak often now of an age of consolidation."

" But not of stagnation," he said, wary of too much conservatism. " We must move."

" Indeed you must! The world moves. You with it — inevitably."

He sat very upright in his chair, cheerfully determined to test the oracle, partly because it would please her to be tested, partly because he was a little superstitious to-night. " May I ask : in what direction ? "

She hesitated, not for her reply, but, he knew well, in diplomatic doubt whether to speak it. She sipped her wine.

" I am an old Englishwoman. May I really try to answer that ? "

" Why, please ! "

" Then — in the direction of responsibility," she said, " of responsibility within your destiny, seen, understood, accepted by your people. The responsibility against the barbarians that Rome failed to hold and that has at last become too heavy for us alone. With this distinction : when Rome failed, renaissance was still possible. If you and we and Western Europe fail — none. The barbarians, once triumphant and backed by modern weapons, can never be overthrown from within. If you and we fail now, Christianity and all other freedoms of the human spirit will be trodden down, out of hope and out of memory."

" ' Responsibility within our destiny ' ? " he repeated. " Will you translate ? Destiny's a difficult word for me."

" You went westward across the Atlantic," she answered, " then westward across your own continent ; others followed, not of English blood, from every nation of the world, to become American, away from their first homes ; always westward, away from Europe and her struggles and confusions. It was like the consistent movement of a great salmon up-river. Now geographically there is no further to go ; now spiritually there is no further to go — *that* way. The time has come to return, as it comes to the salmon. Destiny, which sent you out, is drawing you back again."

" And responsibility ? "

" For democracies — desperately hard. First : to know what it is and where it lies — from day to day, from hour to hour."

" Next ? "

" To accept it — rather than bread and circuses. Hardest of all : to require others to accept it. There are no exemptions. Democracy is not an almshouse, even for the common man."

" And then ? "

" To act — in time. Having acted, rightly or wrongly, not to regret but to pay. Having paid, not to ask the price back. In action — above all, in thought — not to wish to have it both ways."

The dialogue had made a circle round him and Mrs. Muriven. He did not know that others had been listening. Marie said quietly :

" It is true. Our responsibilities, within our destiny, select us ; not we them ; they select us — often quite suddenly. It is like walking into a room that you expect to be empty and finding a man there, waiting for you and looking at you." Then she added : " Always you recognize him, but sometimes at first you call him by the wrong name."

Sturgess knew by a communicated vibration of her personality as she spoke that her mind had been drawn back into the granary at Blaise. Julian's eyes, with that intensification of their blueness which was a sign in him of extreme imaginative activity, were bent upon her. Then a brief silence. Out of it, Valerie said :

" And yet one is always incredulous." She had crossed a bridge of thought independently and spoken from the other side. Looking back, she said: "I'm sorry. I suppose that doesn't make sense. I mean: one supposes that certain things won't happen to oneself. Even those that must happen. We have an idea that *we* are exempt. Even from death. It's against all reason that we should be, but I believe that in our heart of hearts we are all incredulous——"

"Incredulous," Julian said, as if he were affirming what he saw rather than echoing what he had heard, and in a tone so flat and quiet that she continued without a break:

"— of death, seen in the distance."

Julian challenged her: "Why 'in the distance'?"

Perceiving herself to be on unknown territory, she flinched, took alarm, as a child will, not knowing what blunder she had made, what nerve she had touched: "Isn't it so?"

"Indeed it is. But not only so. Not 'in the distance' only! Seen close. Seen close. Why not? . . . But that is the very word: *incredulous*." Then, catching the echo of his own vehemence, seeing her young bewilderment, the flow of colour away from her cheek, Julian leaned forward for forgiveness. "But I'm sorry. I interrupted you. I leap off down a side-track and then shout back at innocent people who can't have been expected to follow. Bad habit. Bad manners. I do beg your pardon."

Never were amends more gallantly made, or received more gratefully than by the smile of relief, the little shake of her head, with which she cast bewilderment away. All was well, but the air was charged; it was necessary that someone should speak at once the perfect irrelevance — a retreat, not a rout.

Mrs. Muriven had the easy resource of long training. "I'm not at all sure," she said, turning an empty glass by its stem, " that we haven't all been talking heresy in Mr. Sturgess's presence. As one who presumably believes that We the People are masters of our fate, he may regard the whole idea of destiny as monstrous superstition."

How much of that she meant made no odds. It was his cue and he took it at hazard.

" On the contrary," he exclaimed, intending only by a deliberate fling to set them staring and make the conversation flow, " there was a moment in which I felt that I was Destiny itself! "

He was rewarded by their eagerness for a tale.

" What was the moment ? " Valerie asked.

Suddenly his heart misgave him. . . . Battles long ago! . . . If he had a tendency to be an autobiographical old soldier, by heaven he wouldn't let it grow on him, anyhow not among the British! . . . And yet, if Marie and Julian hadn't been there . . . Anyhow, why shouldn't he tell his part of his story, not about Blaise, but about the Belgian farm ? . . .

"— the moment," Valerie said, continuing her question, " in which you felt that you were Destiny itself ? "

He had to go on.

" I guess I said it wrong. It was rather as if — as if Destiny were acting *through* me on the lives and homes of the people below."

" Below ? "

He had to go on, but would carry it lightly. Julian and Marie needn't watch him and tauten.

" Below the hill," he said, " on which, very much to my surprise, I happened to be sitting."

He was thinking of Heron, for this was the story which, if he told it, would lead to his meeting with Heron, and he looked at Valerie, her head held high and a little turned, interested, he knew suddenly, not only in the story itself, but in the story because it was his. She was wearing a snaky necklet of plain gold. It had slipped; its small oval clasp, set with tiny sapphires, lay in her throat's hollow, and the shadow of it, pierced by fragmentary fires of blue, turned with her breathing.

"Where was the hill?" she asked. "Why were you sitting on it?"

She had spoken easily and he answered easily: "I had unfortunately dropped on to it out of the sky."

"And a very appropriate entry," Julian cut in, "for anyone about to play the part of the immortal gods," and would have led the conversation away. At the same instant, Marie rose and took the ladies out. Sturgess and Julian followed them, through the porch into the open.

"Do I know that bit of the tale?"

"I think not. It's very early. It has nothing to do with Blaise itself, Julian."

Julian made no answer. On the lawn, when coffee was distributed and cigarettes were alight, it was Mrs. Muriven who insisted that the story should be told. Neither Julian nor Marie now offered any resistance. Because they know, Sturgess wondered, that Heron's name need not be spoken?

10

"IT was in 1943," he began, "early summer. At the time, I was working with British bombers. I had flown out from England on a night raid, and been shot down. I didn't see the others again, though two of them survived as prisoners. For how long I was unconscious on the ground I don't know. I remember very little from the time my parachute opened until I woke with the sun in my eyes, bitterly cold, and in so much pain that I had an idea my body was broken, and lay still. It was a kind of humiliation, after lying still so long, to discover I wasn't broken at all. Under protest, my head and my arms and my legs did what I told them. So I sat up, feeling a fool; then crawled a bit on all fours uphill in the direction of a copse, but that was more of an effort than was pleasant and I soon lay down again.

"It was early morning by the shadows — you know how it is, when the sun is bright but not hot, a pale straw-colour, and you come down to breakfast and say: it's going to be smoking hot later on. It gave me the feel of a holiday-sun, as though I were a small boy who had started out early and had all day ahead. I was happy that way — light-headed, I guess. Anyhow, I forgot for a bit how old I was, and where I was, and why; then remembered; everything became desolate and faded out; but I came back with grass tickling me and the smell of earth in my nose.

"The sun was higher by then and I began to crawl.

What made me weak, or seemed to, was that I wanted to laugh: the way you want to laugh in a dream at something that seems funny then but has no point afterwards. It seemed like a bit of nonsense verse to fly in the air at one moment and crawl on the earth the next."

When he had said this, he was silent for a moment, staring at the grass of the lawn over hands clasped in front of him; then, with a deprecatory smile, he looked up and continued: "Yes, I know it's flat now. It is to me. But at the moment it told me exactly why it didn't matter to Methuselah whether I was alive or dead. However, I went on crawling. One does, for want of anything better to do. I was going to reach that copse if it killed me, and I did. Then I sat down to invent reasons, and found that I had taken cover. That gave me a military feeling which can be a pretty useful drug, as Julian knows better than I do. I propped my back against a tree and began to wonder, not what I wanted to do, but what was expected of me. Rather a comfort, seeing there wasn't a thing I did want to do."

"Had you any notion where you were?" Valerie asked, and her voice took him by surprise, for he was living in the scene again and had almost forgotten that he was describing it. Now he looked at her and, beyond her, at the falling country which began so abruptly at the edge of the Wyburtons' lawn.

"I knew how far we had come out of England," he replied. "Below me was a village straggling along a straight road, which I took to be Belgian. A part of the village climbed a little way up my hill. Nearer to me than this — perhaps a mile from the village and half a mile from my copse — was an isolated house, flanked by outbuildings, evidently a farm-house. I could see a woman in black moving in front of it, hanging out clothes on a line. I decided — well, I'm not sure that I did decide, but it was quite clear to me — that I must take my chance with her. Either she would give me up or conceal me. But I had to wait until dark, and, to encourage myself, ate and drank a little from the supplies I carried with me."

His recollection of that day was less of anxiety than of extreme loneliness, as though the whole universe had become a vast railway station in which he was lost and everyone hurried past without seeing him, and no one heard him when he spoke. The turbulence of a railway station had always been to him an image of terror; it had invaded his mind on that Belgian hill, but the incongruousness of the image and the fact — of the clashing voices, the swirling anonymity of a myriad travellers, and the placid emptiness of his hillside — was an incongruousness that words would not bridge, and his narrative halted. As his listeners were silent, he said lamely: "I didn't know what to do next," and, after a long pause, continued: "But I'll tell you what I did do. I fixed on a sentence in French and said it over and over again." Then he sat back in his chair, came clean out of the past, and looked at Marie. "Marie knows what my French is like. Anyhow, it hasn't a powerful English or American accent. Give me a sentence and I can *say* it. The trouble is to get the sentence. It's the same with my German. I can read both languages pretty well, but, when I talk, finding words is like looking for water in a drought. So I spent all day rehearsing what to say when the door of that farm-house was opened to me. The sentence became hateful, I said it so often. It became a kind of doom that I was pronouncing on the people down there."

The word "doom" echoed ridiculously in his mind when he had spoken it; "pronouncing doom" — fat, pompous words! "What I mean," he explained, looking at Valerie, "is that I knew I had become, for them, what you call an 'agitator', and I believe that now, the world being tormented as it is, to leave men in peace has become a supreme virtue. My arrival would be a curse to them, another disturbance of their normal peaceful life. They had been invaded once, poor devils, and had made their adjustment to it, and here was I, with my infernal sentence and my foreign uniform, a new contradiction of what decent sanity and continuity was left in their day-to-day existence. I began to see their home with their eyes — the table set for a meal, the clock ticking as it had in peace-time, the windows looking out on peaceful, familiar scenes — and I thought: here am I, hidden in this copse, waiting to bring more trouble on them. If I chose to knock at another door, the people in *my* farm-house would be left in peace. Why should I choose them? All day I watched the woman's comings and goings with a horror of myself, as if I were going to strike her.

"That, maybe, is what Destiny feels like. . . . One imagines with compassion, then acts ruthlessly. Someone has got to take it. . . . Perhaps it is the same with your immortal gods."

He looked at Julian, but Julian was softly tapping his pipe out on the grass. "When dark had come," Sturgess continued, "I went down to that house and knocked loudly and once only, in the hope that any passer-by who heard would not recognize the sound as door-knocking. The woman who opened it could see me clearly enough in the light coming outwards. She stared at my uniform, then at my face. Her hand went up to her throat, but she wasted no time. 'So soon,' she exclaimed at once, as though she had been expecting me. Then, before I could speak: '*Entrez, vite.*'

" There were, I suppose, other houses of that village where I should have received the same treatment. Probably Marie knows; I guess the small tributaries of the River Line were by that time pretty widespread. Madame — I don't know her name even now or where she lived — concealed and fed me for three days. The organization then began to work. She knew what she had to do with me, and when. She told me to be ready to move on the fourth night. I asked where I was going, but she said she didn't know, and that, I think, was true. I was to go in a truck, she said, which would stop beside the gate at the bottom of her field at one in the morning. The driver would say: 'Do you want a lift?' I would answer: 'Yes.' He would ask: 'Are there two or three of you?' I would answer: 'One only.' Those words and no others. I was to climb in over the wheel and crawl into a little house made of packing-cases which I should find in the truck. From that moment onwards I was to do without question and at once whatever the driver told me.

" At twenty before one, I shook hands with my hostess and her son and I tried to thank them, but they made no response. They appeared to be without any emotion except a determination to do their duty and a desire to be rid of me. When I wrote down my name and my address at home — I had hopeful ideas of being able to say thank you in some way after the war — the woman looked at what I had written, shook her head as if she didn't want even to remember it, and burned the paper at her lamp. I suppose what I was looking for was a sign of her feeling emotional towards me, anyhow for some personal dramatization of the thing; but she gave no such sign; and I remember thinking, half an hour later, as I lay among the packing-cases in the truck: these European women don't see themselves as actresses in any play. They are through with that. . . . This woman was like a creature of the Greek Chorus, not a protagonist. She was *in* the play, but she hadn't even a named part, if you see what I mean."

" I see very clearly what you mean," Marie answered.

Sturgess smiled. " I thought I'd hit on something, the way you do when you're a student, and I carried it a bit further. As the truck rumbled on, and branches of over-hanging trees were scraping over my packing-cases, I made the learned discovery that the appropriate chorus was that of *The Suppliant Women* of Aeschylus. What put that into my head I don't know. But I was mighty pleased with it. It seemed to me I had hit on a major truth about Europe — and maybe I had."

" What truth ? " Julian asked.

" That what we call romanticism isn't as false as we have taught ourselves to believe. Anyhow the debunking and de-dramatization of life can be carried to an extreme at which life becomes just animalism and endurance, or just intellect and endurance, and nothing else. I've always thought that Madame Bovary wasn't such a fool as Flaubert made out."

" So did Flaubert," Marie put in. " If he hadn't been a passionate romantic himself, *Madame Bovary* would have been as dull a book as its imitators. It was precisely *that* which banked its fires and made it glow."

It crossed Sturgess's mind uneasily that her and Julian's interruptions were intended to divert him from his story, but he decided that his suspicion was unreasonable. There was nothing secret about this ; it concerned no one but himself ; and he went on, telling of his journey in the truck which, conveniently escorted by two other trucks that had somewhere joined it, halted at last in what, when he was told to come out, he found to be an arch or tunnel running in on street-level under the upper floors of a building. This building seemed to be a factory or warehouse. An elevator with iron gates came down, not to ground-level, but to an iron platform from which goods might be easily unloaded from the trucks, and, farther along the platform, was the mouth of a chute for the discharge of bales that had not to be carefully handled. At that hour of the morning the elevator was out of action, and the driver of his truck, whom he did not see again, told him to climb up the steel ladder beside the chute and knock on whatever he found above him when the ladder ended.

He climbed in darkness and knocked. The blocks of a tackle began to creak, a horizontal gash and two broadening triangles of light appeared as a huge trap-door swung upwards, and he emerged into a shadowy room, where white morning looked in over the shoulders of bales, piled high and contained in a reddish waterproofed material that glinted. Where there were not bales there was furniture, tables standing on tables, chairs on chairs, carpets, rugs, crockery, kettles, stoves. A strong, clean, fusty smell — of ironmongery and almond-smelling wax.

When he looked behind him, he saw a bearded and elongated young man with a long grey apron that gave him the appearance of a rubber tube, who by means of the tackle was now lowering the trap-door into its place. As soon as this was done, the tubular young man took Sturgess's arm and led him down the room. Here, putting his shoulder against an up-ended bale and wrapping his arms about it as far as they would reach, he gave it a twist of a few inches — enough to open an aperture through which they both passed. Sturgess found himself in a little clearance among the bales. The floor was thickly covered with empty sacks and in one corner were bread, water and a bundle of clothes. He was ordered to put on the clothes. His guide watched him while he did so; then produced from within his apron and held out for him to read, a card on which was written in English: "Do not come out. Do not look out. Do not speak or sleep. Wait. Obey." The young man picked up the discarded uniform with all that it contained, and went.

After what may have been a couple of hours of silence, the room outside the enclosure began to sound with footsteps and voices, with the thud of heavy objects and the grindings of trolley wheels. From time to time the elevator-doors clanged. The work of the place went on steadily. During two periods of the day, German voices spoke French.

Sturgess's paramount desire was for sleep; he did not understand why this was forbidden, but, determined to obey, stood or sat upright, not risking to lie down. Once, while he was seated, a sway of his body dragged him back from the very abyss of sleep, and he heard, like an echo in the distances of his mind, the sound of his own thickened breathing. He understood then the reason for the command given him: that he might snore. Tired of standing, he went upon his hands and knees, and kept moving until the burden of sleep was gradually shaken off.

So the day passed, business in the great room ceased, the iron doors clanged for the last time, darkness fell, and all was silent. The tubular youth, presumably a night watchman, now appeared, and, telling him to follow, led the way by the light of a carefully darkened lamp to a small office built of wooden partitions in a corner of the room. Its single window was blacked out and a powerful electric bulb, held in a conical shade of tin, threw its light directly down on to a high, sloping desk on which Sturgess's possessions, extracted from his uniform, were laid out. Before the desk, on a high stool with a back and arms, was a man of some fifty years with very short hair turning grey and rimless glasses set low on his nose. He looked at Sturgess over these glasses, smiled thinly and held out his hand, as a polite surgeon receives a patient. "I regret," he said in good but extremely careful English, "we have kept you so long. You came on what we hoped would be a convenient day, but it was not so. You will be hungry. There is wine and food on that tray. You can eat while we talk." Sturgess seated himself on another stool and began to eat. He said that he would rather drink water than wine if he was to stay awake, and was told that, in half an hour, he might sleep the clock round.

He was subjected then to a careful examination. He was asked of his home, his school, the date of his leaving the United States, details of his stay in England and of the aircraft in which he had flown. The technical questions he refused to answer, and they were not pressed. Instead, he was asked to imagine that he had come down the steps of the United States Embassy in London and wished to go to Rainbow Corner: would he please describe the route? He replied without difficulty. On the morning before his last flight, what English newspaper had he read? He said: *The Times*. What was the principal item of news on its front page? But, he answered, it doesn't carry news on the front page. Surely, in the last four months it has done so? No. . . . His questioner shrugged his shoulders: "You will find hot coffee in that flask," he said. "Will you take a cigarette?"

Sturgess checked himself with the cigarette between his fingers. "No," he exclaimed, "yours are precious. You have one of mine," and he clapped his hand to the place where his cigarettes should have been, only to find there the shabby, ill-fitting civilian jacket that had been given him in the morning.

"The cigarette," the grey-haired gentleman answered, "is one of yours. I accept your hospitality. . . . Now will you kindly answer these further questions?"

Slowly Sturgess understood their drift. They were all directed to the United States as it had been when he left or to England as it was a month ago. They were not technical questions, the answers to which could be of value to an enemy. If he understood any one of them in a technical sense and refused to answer, it was dropped. The current slang, the current entertainments, the cost of postage or of a seat in a theatre, were what interested the questioner.

"But look," Sturgess said, "are you doubting that I have been in England at all? Don't my papers say who I am? Didn't I fly out? Wasn't I shot down? Isn't that how I am here?"

"Yes, my friend, but it is also how an enemy, *un faux Anglais*, a false Englishman or a false American, would wish us to believe that he came here. Do you understand?"

"No, monsieur, I do not understand. If the enemy knew enough to be smoking a cigarette with you here, he would know enough to hang you."

"That is true. But he would not know enough to hang all those through whose hands you will, I hope, successfully pass on your way into France and Spain. He would wish to pass himself into the Line and through it, would he not? He would wish to be what, in the River Line, we speak of as 'a barge'. . . . I assure you, sir, it is very necessary for us to be cautious — the more so because time always presses, time always presses ; we can't keep people long here, at headquarters ; we have to reject them or send them forward. And so we do our best. We try to divide people into categories : they are ' a hundred per cent safe ', or ' eighty per cent ', or they are ' accepted with reserve ', or ' with great reserve '. We send these notifications down the Line. You understand ? "

" Yes," said Sturgess, and grinned. " How many marks do I get ? "

" Shall I tell you ? Eighty."

" Eighty ? But surely to God I'm safe enough ? "

The surgical gentleman smiled. " You are not an enemy agent," he conceded, " but you are an amateur, my friend. Let me explain." He took off his glasses and polished them. " I have said that, from the point of view of the River Line, you are a ' barge '. Now a barge, Mr. Sturgess, is a vessel without initiative. It has no engines of its own, no masts, no sails. It is towed from place to place. Often, because the time to move it farther has not come, it rests for a long time in one position, as you have done to-day. It rests patiently, silently, passively. You are, in that sense, a barge. Is it understood ? . . . Very well. One other thing is to be understood. You have no knowledge of the conditions by which your journey will be governed. None. You will seldom know where you are or where you are going. Your judgment in any emergency will be valueless. You will therefore not exercise it. At each stage of your journey, you will pass through different hands. Sometimes the person who has charge of you will appear to you timid or rash or unintelligent, sometimes tyrannical or, simply, fussy ; often that person will be less well-educated than yourself. From time to time, it will become manifest to you that that person does not know, in fact, why he or she is doing, or is commanding you to do, such and such a thing. Nevertheless, you must obey — even in small, humiliating things. They are always the hardest, as Rousseau well knew. It is very hard for an amateur to obey. If suddenly it should be said to you: 'Spit', you must spit. If it should be said: 'Fall down in the mud', you must fall instantly. If the order is: 'Sleep', you must nod and snore a little. And if, as might happen, your presence should endanger your companions, and you should be told to get out of the truck or the train on which you are travelling and disappear, you must take that chance also. A barge may be left behind, if the tug is overloaded. Is it understood?"

"Yes," Sturgess answered.

"And you are not accustomed to discipline of that — I will not say slavish — of that absolute kind? Those who obey in free countries obey what they understand to be reasonable orders — is it not so?"

"Yes," said Sturgess, "but Belgium and France also are free countries."

"They were, my friend." There was a long pause. "But we are reduced, as you see, to the conditions of conspiracy. You are an amateur in conspiracy: an amateur in war. I mean, you have not that power of being able, on occasions, to *identify* reason with obedience which professional seamen and soldiers assimilate into their blood. Therefore, I am afraid, only eighty per cent." He lifted his shoulders apologetically. "In any case, I am bound to ask you to take an oath; not personal to you; all take it; I have taken it. . . ." He produced a varnished card with writing on it. "Will you read it quietly first? Then, upon your God and upon the honour of your country and upon your love for your friends, swear it aloud? I do not conceal from you," he concluded, carefully readjusting his glasses, " that it is a surrender of will and judgment. It requires you, if necessary, to kill or to die. Such are the absurdities to which collective thought reduces us when carried to a logical extreme."

11

At this point in his narrative, Sturgess paused, looking round him at the English evening as though he were a little surprised to find it there. How much of what he remembered he had put into words he knew but indistinctly, for, as one's eyes sometimes become fixed upon a light and blinded to all that surrounds it, his mind had been fixed upon the shrewd, dry man who cross-examined him; and the scene had so replayed itself in his imagination that his retelling of it had become very little a deliberate act.

In the same way, that part of his mind which had remained aware of his audience on the Wyburtons' lawn had been fixed on Valerie Barton to the exclusion of the rest. While he was speaking, she had watched him steadily, leaning forward in her deck-chair, and he had felt that when the time came for him to leave the office where the oath was administered and to go on the next stage of his journey, she might almost appear as a character in the narrative itself. This was fantasy and confusion; he shook himself free of it; but there had been, he knew, a continuous communication between him and her of which the others knew nothing, and his sense of this communication, his certainty that every sound and scent of that night was quickened for her also, filled him with a mingled confidence and awe, so that every common experience was shot through with a rain of arrowy light; the touch of air upon his face, even the glaze of china under his fingers when he lifted his cup from the grass, was delicious; and to him, held in suspense between the remembered and the actual, as though between sleeping and waking, it seemed to be a miracle of proximity that his eyes, which had yet to read the words of the oath set out on a varnished card, should hold in their view her wrist and hand, stretched beyond the knee where her arm rested, and that the fingers he saw should, as he became silent, close.

"What were the words of the oath?" Mrs. Muriven asked.

"They are just words," Marie said at once, but he had not needed her restraint. It was enough for him that, when the oath was taken, the Belgian had led him down a flight of iron stairs, through a short passage which seemed to be an enclosed bridge over a street, into another building; and that there, in a room like a waiting-room, with old railway-posters crinkled on its wall and three mattresses on its floor, he had for the first time set eyes on the boy and the man whom he was afterwards to call Frewer and Heron. He wouldn't speak of Heron now.

"I don't think I remember the words," he said politely and untruthfully. "In any case, I have drifted on far beyond the point when Destiny sat on a hillside and looked so solemnly down on the people below."

Not long after this they moved indoors, and walked through the dining-room into the library beyond it. On the way Valerie said to him:

"Why are you afraid of your story?"

"Afraid?"

"Mr. and Mrs. Wyburton are. You, too — or—" She looked into his face questioningly.

"Or what?" he prompted her.

" Or didn't you know until now that you were afraid of it ? "

" I don't think I am. I don't think I am," he repeated, " except that, for various good reasons, I don't want to force it on *them*. They know it too well. . . . But there's something," he added, " I should like to say to you before we follow them in. May I ? "

They were in the dining-room. Though there had been daylight still on the lawn and the curtains were back, no colour was left in the pictures, and the looking-glass was black as a night-sea burnished with the reflections of a shredded sky. At Sturgess's question, she, who had been moving slowly across the looking-glass towards the library door, became still. Light from the doorway, falling ahead of them, drew up a honey-coloured gleam from the floor-boards ; and behind her, before the mirror and within it, sickles of watered light shone from branches of a candlestick.

Her voice asked : " What were you going to say ? "

" That . . . you seemed, while I was telling it . . . sometimes, a part of the story."

She hesitated, and, he thought, sighed. " Everyone feels," she answered, " that they have known . . . the other person before." Then, understanding suddenly how much she had acknowledged, she looked straight into his face for a moment before moving past him into the lighted room.

There everything was plainer, and on the surface of manners. When they began to laugh at him because the farm-woman had burned his address and because, they said, his offering it to her was only further proof that his country was a matriarchy, he enjoyed their banter ; and when, continuing it, they asked whether there had been no other occasion on which he had played at Destiny, he said: "Yes, to tell you the truth, I'm playing that game now."

Valerie's eyes moved to him. He observed but disregarded their movement, and, when the time came for the guests to leave, he followed her through the long window of the library and walked with her towards the Ford.

"Do you drive, or Mrs. Muriven?"

"To-night, I do. It tires her with lights. Even she is getting old. She has changed since I saw her. But that was seven years ago — in the weeks before Dunkirk. One forgets how long the war went on."

"Did you know Julian then?"

"Commander Wyburton? No. It wasn't here. I have never been here before. Godmother didn't live here then. It was in Yorkshire, in the house she had shared with my grandmamma, who was German — does that surprise you?"

"You mean: does it shock me? You forget I'm American."

Valerie smiled. "But you know," she said half-seriously, "I'm really more German than one grandmother accounts for. Her family came out of Germany in the 'sixties when she was in her teens, but she clung to that old world, the literature and the language, and she rubbed it into us. She and Godmother used to talk German continually; so did our own mother, so did we. It was quite as much my first language as English. You see, my home used to be in the West Riding and we spent our childhood almost as much in their house as in our own. Then we came south. Grandmamma and my mother both died and we didn't often go north afterwards. But my brother and I went up to see Godmother for his last leave before going to France. Then the war flared up.

It was the last time I saw her — or him."

"But if you go to South Africa——"

"South Africa? . . . No, no," she said impetuously, "not that brother. The South African one is the younger of my two brothers — half-brothers, strictly. It was the elder one who mattered to me. I was five years younger. When I was small, and even now—— But that is of no interest except to me. For everyone else, he's dead."

Sturgess said: "You loved him."

"He was everything. As if we were one. Do you know what I mean if I say we had each other's legends? . . . Have you ever watched a child playing a solitary game? Not a game you recognize. His own secret game. All you see is, perhaps, that he crawls backwards and forwards again and again over the same bit of grass, and touches the same stone as he passes it, or turns it over, or looks at it in a special way. He is performing a legend, and you are outside it, and all his life is inside. And later it's true, I think, anyhow for some people; they build legends into their lives which are — which are," she continued rapidly, "the glow inside quite ordinary things. To be *in* someone's legend is to be loved by them. He was in mine. I was in his. It never occurred to me that he didn't know why I touched my stone or what I said to it or when it was a palace and when a loaf of bread. He wasn't ever strange to me or outside me." She looked towards Sturgess: "How do you say that?"

"I should say: you talked the same language."

She nodded. "But not only the same poetry. The same prose too." She laughed suddenly and happily. "And the same nonsense-rhymes. It was almost — how do I say that? — almost an identification. I used sometimes to feel that I was he, and he was I."

They were standing by the Ford.

" How was he killed ? "

" He was taken prisoner. He was killed escaping. Anyhow, he has never come home. . . . You see, that is why I am going to South Africa ; it's no good staying here. He and I were going to live and work together here after the war. So we planned."

" Suppose," said Sturgess, " that one of you had married. Wasn't that a possibility ? "

She smiled. " Yes. I suppose so. We should have talked the same language about that, I expect. I don't know. I wasn't eighteen."

12

THAT night, seated on the edge of his bed, fully aware of what had happened to him and unwilling to end in sleep this first day of his knowledge of her, he asked himself why she had spoken as she did, why — as he saw it now — she had " so gloriously given herself away ". He retraced their conversation for the joy there was in retracing it, and because there was a streak of earnest precision in him which wanted to understand everything.

His saying that she had " seemed a part of his story " had clearly been an attempt to strike below the surface of acquaintanceship and to establish a personal link between them. It had been, as he now cheerfully and even triumphantly confessed, a deliberate " emotional opening ". Touched by her beauty held in the darkness of the looking-glass, and knowing that his time was short, he had taken his chance. If she had repulsed him then, he would have been neither discouraged nor surprised. Her intuition, he was sure, had been to ride away from the personal on some evasive generalization. " Everyone feels . . ." she had begun, and perhaps had not known how her sentence would end. But what she had said was: " Everyone feels that they have known . . . the other person before," and that sentence, having slipped out, had no possible meaning unless by " everyone " was meant " everyone who falls in love ". She could not take it back or cover it. Being honest, she had not made the vain attempt.

In fact, he thought, nothing new was acknowledged by her words. Our minds and bodies and the air we breathed had made that acknowledgment hours earlier.

I knew then, he said to himself; I know now, as I sit here, that her being and my own have run together as streams run together; and yet I am incredulous. He understood suddenly, with understanding that pierced him like a knife, that when, having spoken beyond her intention, she had lifted her head and looked steadily at him, she also had been incredulous with that incredulity of what is certain which, she had said at dinner, we all have — we all have. . . .

He rose from the bed and drew back the window-curtains, trying to recall her words. . . . I believe, she had said, that we are all incredulous of death, seen in the distance. . . . And Julian had said: Seen close, seen close. Why not? . . .

When Julian had said this, he had been thinking of Heron: " incredulous " had been the look on Heron's face at the last. The word repeated itself in Sturgess's mind while he undressed, and, after he had put out his light, he propped himself on his elbow to stare at the night-sky and to wonder whether the things that we accept easily are not less real than those that take our breath away by their sudden, overwhelming certainty. To know, as he did, that this girl, a stranger, was no stranger, but would love him, was in the same category of knowledge with his knowing that he would die. Truth is verified, he thought, and given authority and depth, by the element of wonder in it, as legends are. As legends are, his mind whispered as he lay in darkness, and, because his thought was an echo of her words, he tried, in accordance with modern precept, to reprove himself for sentimentality, and failed, being plainly in love. Each truth, of his love, of his death, of his being now alive, rose up to him from a spring deeper than his childhood, as peacefully as the thought that he would awake to a July morning — of which also he was, in the instant of falling asleep, happily incredulous and certain.

Soon afterwards he was in the room like a waiting-room; he had been there several days, and was watching Heron's face, with which by now he was familiar.

13

THE Wyburtons' house was set on a ledge on a wooded hill which rose steeply behind it and stretched round its western end an embracing arm clothed with beech, elm and sycamore. Into these high woods and the rolling country beyond, Marie and Julian and Sturgess walked that Sunday afternoon. It was such a walk as Sturgess most enjoyed, swinging and steady, with long stretches of easy companionable silence, from which conversation came up spontaneously. Whatever the subject, Marie's intelligence gripped and ordered it, while Julian lightened it with brief comment and laughter from a cloud. Sturgess's own behaviour on the previous evening was not exempt. They accused him of having told his war-story to enrapture the younger lady, not to inform the elder, and of having succeeded; and so released him to talk of Valerie, and to be laughed at on her account, and to hear her discussed and praised: which, at the moment, was the friendly ballast that his adventure needed. Evening church-bells were ringing through full sunshine as they came homeward.

Julian turned aside into a neighbouring farm, having business there. He would, he said, follow them home, and Sturgess and Marie went on into the lighted woods.

"Happy?" she said.

"Very."

"Then let us sit here a little while. This wood on a

Sunday evening is a good place to be happy in. I am happy too."

"I'm glad, Marie."

"Did you doubt it?" she asked.

"Not since I've been here. I confess I did before I came."

"You mean, in America? It surprises me a little that, in America, you should have troubled your head about me." When he was about to protest, she went on rapidly, silencing him. "No, Philip, don't say what you were going to say. I know that you are, naturally, grateful for what I did for you at Blaise, but that was . . . a Service incident . . . in which we happened to meet—"

"Ah," he said, "you and Julian, the French and English of your kind, you take a professional and Service view of everything. You make it a rule, stricter and stricter since the world began to fall about your ears. You behave as if heroism were not heroism, as if feeling were not felt. Oh yes," he admitted, "I know you feel. But you won't ever acknowledge it. You clip yourselves into your professional reticences as if they were a pair of stays that won't let you breathe or——"

"Go limp," she said.

"Well, yes, but why can't you relax? Isn't it an affectation not to?"

She shrugged her shoulders. "A habit, perhaps. It may be valuable as things become worse."

"But, Marie, there may not be another war in your time."

"Even it that were true, it isn't what I meant."

"What did you mean?"

"A valuable habit. . . . A valuable attitude towards life itself, not ever — as Julian says — to 'spill over'.

There are enough people spilling enthusiasms and grievances in this world, and spilling them in violence, to make it desirable that——"

As she did not finish her sentence, he said: "Still that's no reason to expect me to think of our meeting at Blaise as impersonally as a parcel might think of its meeting with a postman."

"No, Philip, I see your point," she replied with the smile she might have given to an eager boy. "But don't forget that I was the postman. You will agree that it is desirable for a postman to train himself to think impersonally of his parcels. . . . As I think you know," she added, "I didn't always succeed."

Sturgess watched her for a moment before asking: "You mean Heron?" Her silence assented. "Tell me, Marie, straight out, now: you would rather not speak of him?"

She shook her head. "Now we are here alone, it would be a relief to hear you speak of him to me. . . . I don't know that I have much to say. I don't, honestly, know."

He had wanted to ask questions; now they wouldn't come. He picked up a stone from between his feet, rolled it from hand to hand, then tossed it into the brushwood downhill.

"Last night I dreamed of him."

"Yes," she answered gravely and unsurprised, "last night our minds were full of him. What did you dream?"

"We were in that room like a waiting-room outside Brussels. What was that room, Marie?"

"I don't know. I was never there. Perhaps the outer-office of what was once a travel bureau? Does it matter?"

"Anyhow," he said, "I dreamt of that. He and Frewer and I were examining the photographs that were to be attached to our forged papers. That was memory; we did, in fact, examine them, and I remember we had a long discussion about what we were supposed to be — disguises and so on. Whether that came into my dream or not, I'm not sure. What did come in was Heron's photograph — and his face. Frewer said that the disguise in the photograph made him look more like a heron than ever. He leaned back with a pencil held vertical at the length of his arm and measured up the proportions of Heron's head. Then he said: 'It's the height from ear to crown'."

"Is this dream or memory?"

"That bit," said Sturgess, "is both, I think. Frewer was trying to be a painter in private life, a student at some art-school; and I remember his saying: 'It's the height from ear to crown' and our discussing what hat would conceal it. But what I *saw* in the dream was — well, it seemed to be the essential character of Heron's appearance — not just tallness but a kind of movement upward so that, in some extraordinary way, even when he was in a chair or seated upright on the floor, and much more when he was walking, you felt that he was, physically—" Sturgess paused before the word and gave it an interrogative tone: "— light?"

"That," she said with the odd primness she had sometimes when she was deeply moved, "is exact. Light. Not burdened. Not tethered."

He loved that primness in her; and the better because it made him laugh at the same time that it conjured up for him the unassuming, indomitable spirit of the schoolmistress who, for week after week and month after month, had taken strangers into her house at Blaise, had commanded them and seen them through, had smiled dutifully at the Germans, and, at the appointed hours, had conducted her classes and prepared her lessons. With this in his mind, he said now: "You know, Marie, what beats me isn't so much that you went on teaching at your *lycée*, but — speaking as one teacher to another — that you could sit down in cold blood and prepare."

"I?" she answered. "Now what on earth made you say that? We weren't talking about me. You were telling me about your dream."

"No good," he answered, "dreams can't be told."

"About him, then."

What was it, he asked himself, that she wished to be told about Heron? Was the reason for her having raised the subject now the simple one: that she had, in her heart, loved him, had put away all speech of him since her marriage to Julian and was hungry for the very sound of his name? When one whom we have loved is dead, all account of him from those who were with him when we were not is precious, seeming to extend his life in our memory, which cannot now be extended in our experience. Perhaps this, and no more, was the reason for her asking, and Sturgess talked of Heron readily, pouring out, for his own sake as well as hers, incidents of his and Heron's and Frewer's journey together from Brussels to Blaise. In a sense, Heron had been distinct from them, for they, if they had been challenged, would certainly have been lost, having by no means the language to sustain the parts assigned to them on their forged papers; while he, who was supposed to be a German merchant, travelling to the Charente and the Bordelais for wine and to the Limousin for oak, had seemed sometimes almost to hope that he would be challenged, so confident was he of his German. He, who was the least boastful of men and would say almost nothing else of the tight corners he had passed through on his way from his prison-camp to Belgium, had insisted (overmuch, Sturgess had thought sometimes) on his gift of tongues, acquired, he had said, " in an innocent cradle " and turned to account against Germans. " Overmuch ", because it had led him, while the three of them were on their way to Blaise, to say things that had made even the imperturbable boy, Frewer, touch wood and cross his thumbs.

" In that single respect," Sturgess said to Marie, " Heron had what seemed to us at the time a shocking rashness. Even now, in the light of what we know, it seems to me odd. Once, on a stage south of Paris, we were travelling on a bus. A German picket stopped us, had all the passengers out on the road, and demanded papers. As it happened, the examination wasn't as thorough as it should have been; I suppose they had orders to look for someone in particular; once they were satisfied that the someone was not there, they weren't interested any more; but when it was over and we were free to climb back into the bus again, Heron loitered and began to chatter; he even took one of the soldiers by the arm and led him aside and said something that made him laugh; they parted on a roar of very German laughter — mouths wide open.

" In the bus we could say nothing. Our one concern, when we had to travel in a public vehicle of any kind, was to avoid conversation — though Heron didn't; indeed, we owe him that — he talked time and again to cover our speechlessness. But when we were alone that night under cover again, I did ask him why on earth he had *opened* conversation with the German picket. He smiled and said: ' I like pulling their legs. Besides, if I talk to them, it's the best of all possible ways of preventing them from becoming curious about me.' "

" And that," Marie said, " is of course true."

" True enough," Sturgess said. " Frewer's silence and mine were the guiltiest parts of us. Still, when an examination is over, when you have already been given the all-clear and the bus-driver has restarted his engine, to turn round then and begin to chatter did seem to us like tempting Providence. And that wasn't all. Heron laughed at us for being so solemn about it. He said that a ride in a bus or a train had become an outing for him; the River Line cover was too damnably efficient — it didn't give a chance to his comic talent! Of course," Sturgess added, " at the time, we laughed too. He wasn't a man you criticized for long. When he said that kind of thing, he had — or seemed to us to have — an irresistible combination of confidence and gaiety which, when we were tired and down, gave a lift to the heart like food and wine."

As he said this, Marie, who had been staring at the ground while he spoke, lifted her face to his.

" You say '*seemed* to us to have—'. You say 'seemed' — in the past. Doesn't it seem so to you still? "

" Well," Sturgess replied, " everything looks different if one sees him as — as what we now know him to have been. . . . I mean, the part he was playing——"

" Wasn't it even more dangerous than you supposed? Does that detract from the 'confidence and gaiety' with which — with which he played his . . . comedy part? "

" No," he answered with hesitation, " I suppose not, if you look at it all from his own professional point of view."

" Well," she said, " give the professional his credit still. . . . But tell me," she went on, speaking quietly and with the irony gone from her voice, " when you say he gave you 'confidence', what exactly do you mean? "

" In the first place," Sturgess answered, " he had become, quite clearly, the leader of us three."

" Ah, that I understand ! At Blaise he became, quite clearly, the leader of us five."

Sturgess put his hand for a moment on her arm. " That's for you to say."

" No," she answered, " there's no contradiction in what I say. Nor am I being modest — or emotional. At Blaise, it happened, so to speak, to be my ship. I was in command. I gave the orders. And, after Julian came, as he was senior by rank, he gave orders under me. That doesn't prevent its being true that there was a quality in Heron which——"

" Which made him," Sturgess suggested, " anyhow potentially, a great man."

But she shook her head. " I think you miss the point, Philip. Not great, even potentially, in terms of success. As you said, he gave a lift to the heart ' like food and wine ', but he wasn't a ruler and never would have been. He was one of the people of whom it would have been said at the end of a long life that ' he hadn't fulfilled his early promise ' or that ' he had always let the big chances slip '. He would always have let himself be jostled out of what are called ' the big prizes ', because it so happened that he was independent of them. He travelled light ; he hoarded nothing — not life itself, I hope. I believe that he wouldn't have regarded even death as a loss because he didn't think of life, as most of us do, as a diminishing personal credit at the bank." She had been speaking meditatively, almost prophetically, as if he had been still alive with a future for her to foresee, and Sturgess, his mind suddenly full of the violence of Heron's death, wished to drag her back from so dangerous a mood. But intervention by him was unnecessary. With an act of will that wrenched her whole body, she dragged herself back from it.

"Was it the fact of his being so proud of his German that first made you doubt him?" she asked. "As an enemy agent, wasn't that the very thing that he would have soft-pedalled?"

"Not necessarily," Sturgess answered. "Not on the principle of a double bluff. . . . But, Marie, there's one thing you must understand. I dare say I ought to have suspected him; the indications, except the final overwhelming one, were all there before my eyes; I dare say I was hopelessly guileless or 'unprofessional' if you like; but it is true nevertheless that, all the way from Brussels to Blaise, and for days at Blaise in your house, I didn't suspect him, except—"

He paused to examine the difficult truth of what he was saying, and so difficult did it prove to be that his silence continued until he heard Marie, at his side, repeat the one word: "except?" Was this why she had at last allowed the subject to be spoken of: that she wished to know, precisely, how soon he had begun to doubt Heron and what force, at each stage, his suspicion had had? He wondered why she should wish to know.

Looking at the vast, smooth trunks of the beech trees rising from the escarpment below and towering above their heads, seeing in their intervals the valley brimming and aglow, and hearing about him the quiet murmur of the wood, he remembered the happy expectation with which he had come to this place, an expectation of friendship and peaceful reminiscence which all his surroundings now fulfilled, and asked himself, with a shudder of misgiving, how it was that the past, which had seemed, even in its tragic aspect, to be remote and at rest, was now reaching up towards him. He had wanted nothing so much as to talk of it; now he wanted to cover his eyes from it, to let it go; and he stood up, determined to snap the thread of a conversation which it must be agony for her to continue.

"I've been clumsy," he said. "I'm sorry. I'm like a silly boy with my 'Blaise adventure'. Let's talk of happier things."

She rose with disciplined acquiescence, and walked on behind him. The wood-path was narrow and held them in single file, but soon broadened. She came up with him then, and, to his astonishment, for she was the least demonstrative of women, put her arm in his.

"Poor Philip," she said, "it must have been hard for you — suspecting and not suspecting."

He was convinced that, in spite of the gentleness of her tone, she was inwardly reproving him either for blindness or for indecision — for "amateurishness" at any rate; and this touched him on the quick. "Marie," he protested vehemently, "if I had really suspected, I should have found a way to tell you or Julian sooner. I didn't *consciously* suspect. I suppose I noticed . . . the indications. But they didn't come together, they didn't point to a conclusion, until the very end. Do you believe that?" He was passionately defending himself against the charge which, he felt, her mind was making: that he had concealed his knowledge from her, that he hadn't spoken soon enough. "The mind accepts," he said, "what it is in a condition to accept. For a long, long time, it just refuses evidence against people it loves. It notes the evidence, as I noted, among other things, that he once helped himself to French postage-stamps and once, even, bought them. But I let it go. To me, it simply wasn't credible that he was false. I loved talking to him. I loved being with him. I was thinking all the time of the personal relationship. I let all the indications go — there they were, but I let them go, until, at the very end, they rushed together and, as it were . . . coalesced into a certainty."

This seemed to him, as he spoke it, to be the whole truth and a sufficient explanation of what had happened. Only when he had done, did it seep into his mind that for her also it had " simply not been credible that Heron was false ", and yet, when the evidence appeared, she had acted instantly. Remembering this, he would have defended himself again, but she forestalled him.

" Don't think," she said, " that I am blaming you." A little flicker of a smile passed over her face. " I'm not even accusing you, poor Philip, of ' professional ' neglect."

" What then, Marie ? Something — I mean not his death only, but something else is troubling you."

She did not answer at once, and he knew by her hesitation that she was withholding the answer she might have given. She was visibly tempted, but did not yield. " I expect," she said instead, " it was only that I wanted to hear you say you valued him in that way. I knew it, of course. It's odd : one wants to hear things put into words."

The wood opened out, the lawn was at their feet. On it, looking over the valley, his back to them and the house, was Julian. As they went down, Marie called to him, and he turned with an eager movement, as though he had been lonely or anxious.

" You have been a long time."

" We loitered, talking."

That he knew they had been talking of Heron, Sturgess did not doubt, for there came into his face that strange mingling of protectiveness and foreboding which, in Marie's presence, the thought of Heron always evoked.

Julian had, on those occasions, a tenderness for her different from his tenderness at any other time; his manner was no less brusque but its brusqueness became a means of communicating the special nature of his love: its admiration, its modesty, its nervous quality of taking nothing for granted — and, Sturgess added, its fear. Of what? Fear for her, but on what grounds?

Julian now looked at Marie with pretended severity, as though he were about to lecture a child.

"You have been talking too much. You are tired out."

"Yes," she said, "I am tired. For no reason, I get tired quite suddenly." She sat on the ground, drawing her feet up under her. "Oh, I wish that part of my pleasure in every pleasant thing — in just sitting here and being peaceful — weren't the negative joy of its not being hell. You and I shall have that all our lives," she said to Julian. "And you, Philip? Not you, I think? You don't live with the feeling that happiness is exceptional — something momentarily, and perilously, almost impossibly, allowed? Do you?" Before Sturgess could reply, she continued: "That, really, is the difference between you and us. It's the answer to your question: 'Why not relax?' We have lived all our lives in a campaign or on the edge of it. I remember no time in which 'security' or the want of it wasn't a public obsession. And now—" She thrust back her hair from her forehead. "Sorry, Julian." She stood up, for an instant took his hand, then dropped it.

"Still," he answered, "we farm our land, my dear."

"Yes."

"Very well, then," he added with deliberate harshness, "that for the time being is our job. Is there any more to be said?"

" No. I'm sorry. Take no notice of me. I'm in a black mood to-night."

Never before having seen her break or bend, Sturgess was silenced. Julian, he thought, would make some attempt to comfort her, but he left her to recover her own poise.

She said: " I am going indoors to sleep for half an hour."

When she was gone, Julian said: " ' For, if thou rest not, busy maggots eat thy brain, and all is dedicate to chaos '." And in answer to Sturgess's inquiring glance, he went on: " That? Oh, it applies to all of us, not to Marie only. ' O proud, impatient Man—' You know it? " And he repeated fast, beating down the rhythm:

O proud, impatient Man, allow to Earth
Her seasons. Growth and change require their winter
As a tired child its sleep. Thou art that child;
Lie down. This is the night. Day follows soon.
Wake then refreshed, wiser for having slept.
This is old nurses' counsel, and the gods',
For, if thou rest not, busy maggots eat
Thy brain, and all is dedicate to chaos.

" And that," Julian added, " may well be what Mrs. Muriven had in mind when she said that America was entering upon an age of consolidation. ' This is old nurses' counsel, *and* the gods'.' "

" I thought you were a naval commander," Sturgess answered. " How do you memorize these things? That ought to be my job."

" Oh," said Julian, " we got leave, you know. . . . Now, let's go and drink while Marie sleeps. Same good reason."

They moved in across the lawn. A large Roman snail,

leaving its slimy track on the grass, was patiently making its way over that green continent. Sturgess would have helpfully picked it up and put it on its way.

" Why ? " said Julian. " Leave the independent beast alone, Philip. It's in no hurry. And you haven't the least notion where it wants to go."

Willingly playing the part of solemn professor, Sturgess, with a broad grin, sat down on his heels above the snail and began to demonstrate, with pointing finger, that he did know where it wanted to go. The curve of its track, if produced far enough, would lead it midway into the rhododendron bush where, presumably, it had means of livelihood.

Julian took him under the arm. He resisted with a shout of laughter, and found himself dragged up.

" Now listen," Julian said. " You give it a chance to change its mind. It may not be wanting to earn a livelihood; it may be living — like your Thoreau.

> What's the railroad to me ?
> I never go to see
> Where it ends.

Same applies to snail-tracks. We can't have you playing at Destiny every hour in the twenty-four. Even Socialists don't direct snails, and what are you — a Republican or a Democrat or the Lord Almighty ? "

14

HAVING for a moment seen behind what he still thought of as Marie's "professional" reserve, and laughed with Julian over the fortunes of the Roman snail, Sturgess felt himself to be more intimately of their company than he had been since Blaise.

He had noticed often that, when Englishmen and Americans were friends, a time came at which their friendship appeared to stand still. They reached the point at which friends of the same nationality begin to rely upon intuition to supply things unsaid; and there hesitated, uneasily aware that their differences of background, of childhood's memories and young values, might, at a depth below explicit acquaintanceship, cause misunderstanding of a kind that could not arise between men of like upbringing. They lacked confidence for the next advance, put out cautious feelers, moved with gingerly, diplomatic tread. Their friendship, not deepening, might evaporate in politeness.

Now, in the days immediately following that Sunday, Sturgess felt that, with Julian, this awkward stage was past. He called twice on Mrs. Muriven, saw Valerie again, and on his return — in Julian's own phrase — "reported progress". They could talk, both seriously and lightheartedly, of her, in a way that steadied his bewilderment, and enabled him, in a letter home, to give an account of Mrs. Muriven's household which, he hoped, would not alarm his mother but at least give her warning of Valerie's existence.

He found, moreover, that, as Julian and he were able to look sentiment in the face without more discretion than an American would use towards an American or an Englishman towards an Englishman, so, also, they could disagree without circumlocution. They discussed Pearl Harbour and Singapore, the Philippines and India.

" Well," said Julian, " you told us we ought to go and we have gone. Now watch the liberties descend — and remember Mrs. Muriven ! "

" Mrs. Muriven ? "

" ' Too much, too soon '."

They did battle on that, and not with cautious avoidances ; each firm in his own judgment and with respect for his antagonist's. Differing, they moved up India together, to find themselves looking across her northern frontiers with not very different eyes.

" Good," said Sturgess, " we differ to agree."

" So be it," Julian answered. " You hold the trumps, and it's your lead."

They were walking through a street of Tarryford together. Beyond the bridge they separated, Julian to climb his own hill homeward, Sturgess to turn down the lime-avenue which led to the small meadow behind Mrs. Muriven's house.

It was his third visit and he had begun to feel at home there. This time he had come without special invitation, and found Mrs. Muriven alone. As she did not offer to tell where her god-daughter might be, he resigned himself to this uncertainty, carried out tea for her to what she called her " shed " — a small wooden house overlooking the landing-stage where her boat was tied up — and settled down to enjoy her company for its own sake. Their table was outside the shed but in the shade of it, and she hitched a great hat of rough straw by its ribbons to the back of her chair. Her fine-drawn cheeks, a firm, delicate jaw, and eyes deep-set under arching brows gave her an air of lively, and, Sturgess thought now, of beautiful, fragility.

A student of the Victorian age, he regarded her, the intimate friend of Valerie's grandmother, as a specimen, and was not blind to her amusement at being so regarded.

" Yes," she said, " I am indeed a Victorian, but it was a long reign, Mr. Sturgess. Mrs. Oliver, Valerie's grandmother, belonged to the middle of it, and I to the end. I was still in my twenties, a young widow, when the Queen died. You mustn't appeal to me for a contemporary judgment on Mr. Trollope."

This troubled him not at all. The Nineties, at the moment, were not in literary fashion; the better reason for him to investigate them; and he had imagination enough to transfer himself to that vanished decade, to try to see Mrs. Muriven as she had been.

" I wonder," he said, " what I should have thought if I had known you then ? "

" If you had had your present mood," she answered with a quick, searching look, " you would probably have been shocked. We considered ourselves extremely advanced. I, for example, was a revolutionary. I am still, though naturally you don't believe it. The materialists of your generation who call themselves revolutionaries ask : ' How ? ' and, sometimes, angrily : ' Why ? ' But not : ' From what origin ? ' or ' To what end ? ' They are concerned with the intermediate questions. We were trying to ask the final ones — and that," she added with a quietly mischievous smile, " is, I expect, why we looked a little foolish sometimes. Real revolutionaries do! "

Sturgess laughed with her, and led her on to Ruskin, to Morris, to Thoreau, even to Newman. What, in the Nineties, had she thought of them? She underwent examination with delight; then said:

" But you know, Mr. Sturgess, responsible individualism is, I believe, arising again among the young. In America, you have never lost it; nor have we; but among us it has been persecuted and ground down. Now it may return. It is independent of class and doesn't think in terms of class-war. It thinks its own thoughts, pays its own losses, and without sentimentality expects others to do likewise. It has no sympathy with mass-minded gamblers who gamble at the pistol-point and kick over the table when they lose. It keeps the rules and doesn't cheat itself at patience."

" Which means? " he said.

" Probity was the old-fashioned word. Not to rob your children's money-box. To acknowledge Destiny and not whine. To have the courage to wait."

" Ah," said Sturgess with a smile, " you mean not to cut down the fruit-trees because a lot of little boys are yapping for firewood. Is that ' cheating at patience '? "

She nodded. " It's a popular form of dishonesty. It makes the cheater feel generous and it wins votes from the little boys until they find that nothing is left, neither wood nor fruit. Then they starve and shiver, both. . . . And so," she said, " if you think in terms of fruit-trees and are prepared to take the responsibility of protecting them, you are my kind of revolutionary after all? "

" About the fruit-trees," he admitted honestly, " I was quoting." It had, in fact, been Heron's phrase.

" From whom? "

" From a man I knew once — in the war."

" A part of the adventure you were describing ? "

" In fact, yes," he answered. " But what made you ask that ? "

" Only that that story is, I think, very much in the back of your mind. You told it as if it were. You seemed to be thinking and feeling it, rather than telling it to us."

" Valerie told me I was afraid of it."

" Perhaps she ought not to have said that."

" But you, too, thought it ? "

" And you ? " Mrs. Muriven gently asked.

" I think I may be half-afraid of it. I wasn't when I came here. Maybe I am now." He clasped his hands behind his head, leaned back in his chair, and gazed at the river and the meadow beyond it, a piece of common land, fringed by a row of very small houses of great age. " You know, when I was in France, war seemed fantastic and so did life in bombed England at that time. I felt, if you see what I mean, that I should wake up and find the old, normal world — the *real* world — going peacefully on. Now I see it differently. That old man on the green, sitting on a bench with his newspaper ; those boys playing — what is it ? — rounders ? The fat dog waddling home. . . . Why, I can't see a dog or listen to birds on a fine day without thinking : ' You don't know that civilization is rotting. You are exempt. You live in a kind of fairy-tale without knowing it.' My mother, too, and the people I know at home belong to one world ; it was the only real world for me once ; now it seems terribly remote sometimes, even when I'm there ; and teaching English, which is my job, and I love it — why, sometimes, the bottom falls clean out of it when I think of Marie Chassaigne going off each morning to teach in her *lycée* at Blaise. I don't know whether I am making myself at all clear. It's the feeling — many of my age have it, I believe — of being somehow caught between two worlds. That's really why I came to England now. Julian and Marie, I thought, married, settled down to farm — they would be a link. . . . Something's wrong. They aren't a link. But—" He felt what he was saying so deeply that he could look at Mrs. Muriven and say it without flinching, "—your god-daughter, in a way, is."

" A link between your two worlds," Mrs. Muriven said; it was an accepting statement not a surprised question.

"You will think that strange; I have known her so short a time."

She considered a moment. " No. I loved my husband instantly. In that way. He was a link. When I was with him, I felt that I was no longer adrift. . . . He was killed in the South African war soon after our marriage. . . . I have been a widow almost fifty years. The link still holds."

The old man on the bench had folded his newspaper, tucked it under his arm and started on his way home. The boys had tired of their game, and were lying on their backs, kicking their legs in the air.

" For me," Sturgess said slowly, " there's another link. The man I spoke of, the one I quoted from — about the fruit-trees and the firewood. That, too, I have begun to grasp fully only since I came here. Perhaps that's why I'm half-afraid of the story, and it may be why Valerie knew that I was. We called him Heron. The Belgian I told you of, when I had taken the oath, took me into another building and into a room like a waiting-room. There were two there already; a very young chap, a boy almost, called Frewer, and Heron. . . ."

15

He was resolved to make short work of the episodes of their journey from Brussels through France, having no wish to represent himself to Mrs. Muriven as a principal character in a story of peril and escape. Instead, he did his utmost to describe Heron himself because it was in Heron that she would, he felt, be genuinely interested if only he could " bring him to life " ; and, as far as appearance and manner were concerned, the description seemed, if he might judge from its effect on his listener, to be competent. It held her attention ; she nodded her head and sometimes interrupted encouragingly. But she was, he knew, waiting for something that he hadn't given — that identity which is not an aggregate but a distillation of the qualities and appearances of a man, and which, in Heron, shone out — or, more truly, drew you in — with rare power.

" And yet," he said, " in spite of all I have told you, he wasn't, I suppose, what is called ' a powerful personality '. Marie said he would always have missed ' the big prizes ', and I expect that's true. It was the fact that he didn't value or judge anything by its outward effect, but did value things intensely in themselves, that took my breath away."

" He did not value things, you say . . . by their outward effect ? " Mrs. Muriven said questioningly.

" I know that's hopelessly general and vague," Sturgess replied, knitting his brows like a boy who has failed at a lesson. " Well, for example, one night our billet was in an inn on a long straight road that ran along the edge of an embankment. The nearest town was some distance away, but there was a railway-works outside it, and our inn's customers were chiefly the railway workmen, and, I gather, during parts of the year, people who came out for near-by fishing or for parties in the inn garden. There weren't parties any more but there was night-work in the railway-sheds, which meant people coming and going and gave cover for us. The customers had their drinks in a front room or in the garden, which looked out on the road. We lived in a room at the back which had a bench with a vice on it, and was full of tools and cans and bits and pieces — part workroom, part gardener's shed, part store-room. It had one grubby window high up, its outer door was ordinarily locked, and it had an emergency exit into the house, so it suited us well.

" On our first evening there we could have no light because the window wasn't blacked out, but we dealt with that next day, and on the second evening the innkeeper's wife gave us three little oil-lamps, of the kind she might use in the corner of a dark passage, about as powerful as half a nightlight. But *three* — that was the luxury of it! We were pretty good sharers by that time, but we had lived at incredibly close quarters for days and days, eating off one plate, or looking over one another's shoulders to read some scrap of an old newspaper, or putting our heads together over the stump of a candle; and those three lamps made us feel separate and civilized. We put down straw and sacking in parts of the room as far distant as possible; we had books — one each, brought in by that blessed woman with the lamps; and Frewer and I settled down to ours. His turned out to be some manual on home-doctoring, which he said he liked better than fiction because it had a section on anatomy. Mine was *Paul et Virginie*; I opened it in the middle and found that, by holding the page right up against my white tulip-globe, I could just read it.

" Heron didn't go to bed as we did. Next to the room's outer door there was a long-legged desk against the wall — what, I suppose, you'd call a cashier's desk: a thing with a sloping lid. He carried off his lamp to that, and stood by it, writing on the back of scraps of paper he had found inside it. ' What on earth are you doing?' Frewer asked, and added one of the rather feeble jokes that become a habit when you're in a jam. ' You can't write home from here,' he said. Heron looked down sideways, with the lamplight coming up under his jaw and all the top part of his head in the dark. ' A poem,' he said. ' Good God,' said Frewer, ' are you a poet as well as a hussar?' ' I don't know yet,' said Heron, and the corner of his mouth curled up in that queer, affectionate smile he always had for Frewer. ' I may be able to tell you later.' He lifted the desk-lid and looked inside again — for a better scrap of paper I suppose; and while he was rummaging, he said suddenly: ' Look what I've found!' What he had found was a couple of envelopes and two or three loose stamps. ' There you are, Frewer,' he said, ' letter home — stamps and envelopes all provided!' "

Sturgess was silent. The stamps and envelopes were the point of a different story, not of the story he was trying to tell Mrs. Muriven in order to make clear what he had meant when he said that Heron didn't value anything by its outward effect. To make that clear he must tell her about the poem and about — but what he saw before him was Heron, with the lamplight striking upward on to his right nostril and on to the knuckles of the hand with which he flourished the envelope; and, though he did not wish to pursue that aspect of the tale, he said: "I shall always remember him, because of things that happened afterwards, holding up, first the envelopes, then the stamps. I couldn't see the stamps, but from the running together of his fingers into a point I knew he was holding something very small. The shadow of his hand on the wall was the head of a duck with its bill sticking out."

As he said this, Sturgess caught the sound of his own voice. He was talking too emotionally, too excitedly; the stamps and the envelopes were of no interest to Mrs. Muriven; and he commanded himself, with almost academic stiffness, to keep to *her* point.

" Of course, we had no idea that Heron was anything of a poet," he said slowly and with studied calm, " and I have no reason now to suppose that he was. I leaned back against my wall with *Paul et Virginie*, quite foolishly happy because I had said to myself that this was ' reading in bed ', and reading in bed was rationed for me when I was a boy — it was supposed to strain the eyes — and it has been one of my peace-time luxuries ever since. After a time, I heard a click of the desk-lid " — his words were quickening again — " and saw Heron — he looked taller than ever because you couldn't see him below the waist in the dark of that room, and the upper part of him seemed to be floating above the little lamp he had hitched to his forefinger — I saw him coming towards us, and, as he wasn't making for his own straw, I thought he was going to sit by me.

" But I was wrong. He sat on the floor, cross-legged, beside Frewer, and asked what he was reading. Frewer showed him and they peered at the book together. Then Frewer came out with: ' I say, Heron, do you really write poetry? ' . . . ' Yes,' said Heron. . . . ' Do you publish it, I mean? Ought I to have heard of it and all that?' . . . 'No, certainly not.' . . . There was a drift of silence after that until Frewer asked with real puzzlement: 'What on earth do you write poetry *about*? Spring and love and so on?' . . . 'About nothing on earth,' Heron answered, 'at least I suppose not. Are you by any chance a musician?' . . . 'I like it,' Frewer admitted, 'but I don't know anything about it.' . . . 'Well,' said Heron, 'music is *about* something, but not in the same way that what is written in words is about something. And there are people who don't need to have even the sound, the physical sound, on the drums of their ears. They read a score silently or compose silently. And sometimes the music composed silently is about nothing that is visible or touchable or audible; it's about something inside Nature and beyond the senses which isn't even thinkable except in music and, I suppose, only imperfectly even in music. It has always seemed to me that poetry moves towards *that* — away from the logic that ties words to appearances. I think that is what Shelley was struggling for at the end — probably he had been always, but I think he knew it more clearly at the end. There's a very odd bit he wrote not long before he died:

> . . . and soon
> All that was, seemed as if it had been not;
> And all the gazer's mind was strewn beneath
> Her feet like embers; and she, thought by thought,
> Trampled its sparks into the dust of death.

In a sense,' Heron said, 'I suppose that poem was about nothing — about something at any rate that language has never yet given a name to, but that poetry might conceivably communicate, and that Shelley was on the track of.'

" Frewer had sat quite still, listening. After a bit, he said : ' I think I see now. I suppose I shan't to-morrow morning. About something, you mean, which is so far *inside* that you have to stop thinking before you can let it come through ? Still, I don't see,' he continued rather sleepily. ' Poetry must be about something. It can't just be about the music you don't hear. . . .' ' Why not ? ' Heron replied. ' Thought without thinking, sound without hearing, truth without arguing, love without loving, loss without losing. Why not ? Isn't that a subject for poetry ? You can call it nonsense verses if you like. . . .' Frewer shifted his lamp. ' Light without shadows,' he said. ' There were chaps who painted like that. Can I see what you have written ? ' Heron handed over some scraps of paper.

" There wasn't a sound while Frewer was trying to fog it out. Heron sat there waiting as if he would have been quite content to wait for ever. And then," Sturgess said, raising his voice sharply, " Frewer said something that brought me back to earth with a jolt. It was one of our fixed rules that we didn't keep or carry anything written, in case it should be left about and get others into trouble, or, if we were ever searched, be found on us. Frewer became practical. ' But if you can't keep this,' he said, ' what's the good of writing it ? ' . . . ' Just to write it,' Heron answered. . . . ' If ever it was going to be published,' Frewer objected, ' or not even published ; if anyone was going to read it, even yourself, afterwards ; but as things are—' . . . ' Better as things are,' Heron said. He took the bits of paper, burned them at the lamp and carefully rubbed the sparks out on the floor. ' I haven't the least desire to keep it or anything. It makes no difference what you keep. The thing was there before you had it and is still there when it seems to have gone.' "

After a pause which Sturgess found necessary if he was to withdraw himself from the sense he had of being even now propped against a wall with *Paul et Virginie* on his knees, and of hearing Heron's voice; after a long pause — how long he scarcely knew — he looked carefully into Mrs. Muriven's face and remembered to ask whether she saw what he had meant about Heron's not valuing things for their outward effect.

"Indeed, I do. What happened then?"

"Nothing, I think. That's all I remember about that night. I expect we went to sleep."

He felt tired suddenly. He wanted to fall back into the scene he had left and find Heron alive there; not talk about it, knowing him dead.

The surface of the river was no longer bright; it had changed its texture to a dark silkiness cut by little eddies that flowed but seemed not to move, so steady was the glint on their convexities; it was, for him, as though the scene were moonlit, and it shocked him to see nothing changed except that, out of a blue sky, a long, fleecy cloud was drifting across the sun. "But now I think of it," he said, "that turned out to be our last night in that place. I don't know where it was. I could never find it again. It's queer to think that it's there now, looking much as it did I suppose, with the long-legged desk still by the door; and that I shall never be in it again. We were roused early in the morning. Transport had linked and we were two hours on our way before daylight."

That was said; they were two hours on their way; there was no need to tell Mrs. Muriven any more of the place they had left behind; but his memory turned back stubbornly. The door had been unlocked and they had gone out: Frewer first, with the innkeeper who stayed to relock the door; he next; Heron last. As he smelt the first gust of open air, he heard the desk click behind him and, looking over his shoulder, saw Heron take the two envelopes and the stamps.

" Of what use were they to him ? " Mrs. Muriven asked.

" I don't know," Sturgess answered.

" Mementos ? He doesn't sound like a man to keep mementos."

" I don't know," Sturgess repeated. " I didn't ask at the time. And afterwards, how could I say, like an inquisitor : why did you take the envelopes and stamps ? "

He was glad that Mrs. Muriven let the subject drop. Why he had not asked Heron, he could not have told her, for he could not tell himself. An incision of memory, a thin, jagged knife, made him cry out inwardly that the click of that desk behind him had made him suspect Heron. But it was not true ; to suspect him had been, then, unimaginable. That Heron had intended to close the desk silently, he had recognized, but it had been a small barren recognition ; it had bred no consequence ; nothing that could be called suspicion had crystallized. And yet it was true that, as they walked together along the edge of the embankment to where a horse-wagon was drawn up under the trees, he had remembered his own cross-examination in Brussels and had wondered what report of Heron had been sent down the River Line. Coming from Germany, he could have had precious few credentials. None. Eighty per cent ? Not as much. Sixty ? 'Accepted with reserve' ? 'Accepted with great reserve' ?

As we walked along the embankment, Sturgess admitted to himself, I did ask those questions vaguely and reminiscently ; I did ask them — that's true. But I didn't suspect Heron ; that also is true. . . . Odd.

16

Sturgess's attitude towards Mrs. Muriven had, at their first meeting, been more than a little guarded. She had seemed to him too much included within the barriers of her class and prejudice, too much of a Brahmin; and though, even then, he had been interested in the courage of her mind and the fastidiousness of her manner, he had put up defences against her. Since then, he had discovered that she had a faculty of putting him at ease, of flattering him by her attention, of drawing him out, and, though he had enjoyed it, his enjoyment had been accompanied by an inwardly knowing smile, and he had remained on his guard against the beguilements of the Old World. This afternoon she had won him, chiefly by her silences, and by the fact that when he had become — as he knew he had become now and then — too emotional and excited, she had not pressed him. In all his talk of Heron, he was conducting a trial of himself, and she had made him feel that she was on his side, not against him.

After they had sat over the tea-table and strolled down to the water's edge, where she had consulted him about the repair of her decrepit landing-stage, during all of which time not a word was said of Heron, she asked for his help in carrying the tea-things back to the house. He offered to wash up for her. She said no; Alice, her daily woman, would be back to give them supper; but, in the end, he and the old lady — the young lady of the Nineties, he thought — washed up together, rivals in efficiency.

It was he who, almost unwittingly, introduced the subject of Heron again.

" In the United States," he was saying, " we hate indifferentism. You ought to be interested in everything around you. You ought to care what happens and make up your mind that everything — a war, or a peace treaty, or an educational programme — ought to produce, and can be made to produce, better results than last time. We are brought up to have that attitude of mind. I have always had it, and I have it still. But it is fairly obvious that things don't always work out that way. It isn't merely that there are failures and set-backs; it goes deeper than that. A failure that is caused by bad organization or a set-back that has its root in some injustice can, presumably, be overcome by a better organization or by removal of the injustice. But suppose the cause of the failures and the set-backs isn't what we think it is? Suppose the cause isn't that we have gone the wrong way about getting the things we want but that we have wanted the wrong things? If we——"

" You are preaching to the converted," Mrs. Muriven said.

" I know I am. But, you see, I'm not fully converted myself. There's part of me — call it the crusading part if you like — that will never be content without results, which *does* value a thing by its effect. And there's another part — a quietist part — that values a thing for what it is in itself. My trouble is that my crusading part says the quietism is, or may be, just selfishness or indifferentism or spiritual pride, and my quietism says that my crusading, with all the best intentions, is a naïve attempt to change a world that can't be changed by any activist effort of ours. The crusading part says it's my job to try and go on trying; the quietist part that the only thing that matters is to find and follow one's own inner light. How to reconcile those two is what I want to learn — and what the world has to learn, I believe — and Heron was the man who might have taught me. They were wonderfully reconciled in him. He was as resourceful and adventurous and bold as a man could well be. Indifferentism was a thing that the toughest extrovert wouldn't have accused him of. He took every sort of risk; he ran right into the 'dust and heat'; and never faltered or turned a hair. At the same time, he could say and mean what I heard him say that night about the poem. It had been before he wrote it; it would be, after it was burned. The loss of it was simply — I don't know how to say it."

"Yes you do," Mrs. Muriven answered. "You repeated his own words. Have you forgotten?"

They had done their work in the kitchen and were coming out of it into the hall. The front door was open. Valerie, who had just come in, was examining a little packet of letters that the postman had brought.

"Which words?" Sturgess asked.

"'Loss without losing,'" Mrs. Muriven replied.

At that Valerie turned. By her eagerness, the swing of her shoulders, the impression that her wide eyes gave of her lying open to all the winds of experience, Sturgess was newly struck. "Whose words?" she asked.

"Mr. Sturgess was telling me about a friend who shared his escape with him."

Shared my escape! he thought, and drew breath to speak. It shocked him to have dragged to the surface of his mind the fact that Mrs. Muriven's knowledge went no further. Had he, then, so successfully hidden from her what, in retrospect, he now saw as an all-pervading element in his narrative, a poison in its blood? Concealing it from her, he had, as it were, suppressed or muffled his own recognition of it; and so anxious was he now not to be dishonest with her, or not to be dishonest with himself, that his breath was drawn to blurt out that Heron had — had by no means "shared his escape" to the end. But he did not speak.

Mrs. Muriven was retelling his story of Heron's poem. She asked him to repeat Shelley's lines; then ran on, in swift summary, to the end. She said nothing of the envelopes and the stamps which could have had no significance for her. Valerie, alight with interest, entered into their conversation, which took flame from her spark. His chance to say what he had been on the edge of saying was missed, not unwillingly.

In the living-room when her godmother had gone out to arrange for his staying to supper, Valerie sat on the window-seat, her body erect, her face, even when she looked fully up at him, inclined downward by the in-drawing of her chin. He listened to her voice, enchanted by its variation of pace, by its ease and resonance, above all by the directness of her address to him which gave to sound almost the effect of touch.

He asked whether she would go on a river expedition with him, perhaps to-morrow? perhaps the next day — if she hadn't been spirited away to South Africa by then? She answered: "Yes. There's a place up-river called Radlett's Island. Let's go there. We can scrape together some food and take a basket."

They talked of America and the different picnics you had there; then suddenly of war, of the possibility of its coming again, of the perilous uncertainty of Elizabethan days and of their own; then of this day now passing.

When she was in mid-sentence — "Push both your hands out of the window into the sun," he said.

She obeyed, not asking why. He watched the sun's life on her hands until she withdrew them. "Now go on. . . . The things I argue about with myself," he said, "you reach out for with — a kind of assurance, as if they belonged to you."

"Belonged?" she asked. "What things?"

He found it not easy to tell her. "What I am struggling for——" he began.

"What are you struggling for?"

He smiled. "You'll laugh at me, I dare say. It sounds pretty Emersonian. I haven't the gift of saying serious things flippantly. Perhaps, with you, I needn't try?"

"No," she answered, "you needn't."

At that he swerved to an opportunity. "Why? Why on earth do you make special conditions for me?"

"Because you are exciting," she said.

A sweeter thing to hear he had not heard. "I? Exciting? Good heavens, in what way?"

"The way that makes you want suddenly to feel the sun on your hands when Queen Elizabeth is in her grave."

"They weren't my hands, they were yours."

"So much the better; you teach suddenly. Are you a good schoolmaster?"

"Probably not. I don't teach suddenly enough. That's what I was trying to say. I don't teach myself suddenly enough. I suppose that the thing I'm struggling for is some kind of reasoned balance between the activities and the acceptances of life, and you — you did when you were speaking about Heron's poem — you speak of that balance — well," he said, "it's damned hard to say. You speak of it hardly at all as a *reasoned* thing. Much more as a thing to be felt, an experience within reach."

"Not within my reach," she said. "Reachable, if you like."

"Very well. But in sight, like an apple on a high branch for which, it may be, as yet, you haven't stature enough. But in sight. . . . You saw Heron's poem while I argued with myself about it."

"But I understand that!" she exclaimed. "To write a poem that no one will ever see and care passionately about it is like fighting in some corner of a battlefield that no one will ever notice. Or praying, not for the sake of the prayer's being answered. Or loving, not for what love takes or even for what it gives. . . . Philip, that's not indifferentism. Why do you think it can be? It's not avoiding the fire or fearing it. It is passing through the burning, fiery furnace without the smell of fire on you. I think your friend——"

"Heron."

"What was he — I mean by temperament? Did he take an optimistic view of the world?"

"No," Sturgess said, "he took a much blacker view of what was going to happen than I did, if that's what you mean, but it didn't frighten him or make him unhappy."

"Making himself eyes," she answered, "with which to see in the dark."

There was something in her tone which caused Sturgess to say: "It's my turn to ask. Who said that?"

"No one you would know," she said with a quietness of tone that made him forbear.

Long ago, ten minutes perhaps, there had arisen in his mind a question so all-embracing, so raw as he supposed, that he had shied away from it. Now he dared it. Nothing in her delighted him more, because nothing was more deeply personal to her, than her golden willingness to commit herself without grey qualifications, and he asked her if she was Christian.

"Yes," she replied; then, after a pause and with the smile that was no more than a deepening of the points of shadow in the corners of her mouth: "I like your questions. They are sudden too!"

"I like your answers."

"Few people nowadays ask such a question. They are afraid to."

"Well, you see," he exclaimed with a flash of arrogance, "I have to risk being thought not subtle enough. I have to take short-cuts. I haven't long to get to know you. When you say 'yes' like that, it's a long stride between you and me."

She rose and walked across the room. "Did you love him — your friend, I mean?"

"Yes."

"That—" And for once she hesitated. "Oh, I didn't know him. You have scarcely told me anything, except of that one incident. It's foolish, I know. The thing's unsayable."

He came near to her and insisted: "What were you trying to say?"

Trembling, she stood her ground: "That your 'yes', too, seemed a long stride between me and you." Then, with an abrupt turn of her head, she asked on a flow of words swift and by intention casual: "Does that make any kind of sense about a man I never knew?"

"Yes," Sturgess said, "it makes sense to me, knowing him and knowing you." Then he added: "Beginning to know you both."

17

At supper and afterwards, Sturgess resumed his tale. He wanted to arrive in the Chassaignes' house at Blaise, for there, until the last day, he had known, or seemed now to have known, a happiness different in kind from any other happiness within his experience. He wished to re-experience it, and, if he could, to understand it fully, as, he had begun to feel, he had not understood it yet.

But he found that, determined though he was to press his narrative forward to this point, certain incidents by the way sucked him in. They also demanded that he should re-experience them and face (or shrink from) the truth at their core.

"Had you money?" Mrs. Muriven asked. "Were you able to buy things — tobacco for example?"

It would have been simple to answer by saying yes, they had always a little money because it was sometimes necessary that they should be separated for a few hours from the agents of the River Line, their "postmen" or their "nurses" as they called them. It would have been easy to add that he and Frewer had been terrified of speaking to anyone and that Heron had acted for them. He began to answer in this general way, but a scene rose in his mind which insisted on being described, and he told how Heron had gone into a shop to buy tobacco while Frewer and he, separated from each other but keeping touch, had sauntered on. "We never bunched," he said, "if we could help it," and he described the scene in detail — the shop, Heron's figure seen through the open door, the old woman's face looking out tight-lipped from the inner shadows; then the street, the passers-by, even the headline of a derelict sheet of newspaper that he had happened to stare at because it looked up at him out of the gutter. There was no significance in any of these details except that they were associated in his own mind with the instant in which he, turning in his tracks and repassing the tobacco shop in order that contact should not be lost, had seen that Heron, as he came out, paused on the doorstep to slide into his breast-pocket stamps just purchased.

This he did not tell.

His whole description of the incident had led up to it and, suddenly, he could not tell it, for, if he had told it, Mrs. Muriven would have wondered, as she had before, why he had not asked what need Heron had of stamps, and to that question he had no answer. So, instead of completing his story, he took up the salt-spoon and, with its edge, began to press the salt into patterns.

In a court of law, he would have been asked: *Did you or did you not at that time regard his buying stamps as a reason to suspect him?* I did and I did not. . . . *Were you afraid to ask his reasons because you doubted them?* I was and I was not. . . . *But that is unreasonable; if one answer is true, the other is untrue; can you not decide?* I cannot decide. . . . *Then there was in your mind an element of doubt — doubt of him?* Not doubt, but fear of beginning to doubt. . . . *And yet you loved him?* Yes. . . . *And yet you "feared to doubt him"?* Yes. . . . *Are the two compatible — to love, to trust absolutely, and to fear to doubt?* Yes, yes, yes. . . . *Are the two compatible — to believe and not to believe?* Yes. . . . *At any rate* (ironically) *you found them so then?* I find them so now. I find them so now. That is the stress of it, the drag and the ache of it! Don't you see, he shouted silently at this inward persistent questioner, that, when once you begin to move on the plane of emotion, reason doesn't answer the bell when you ring?

Under all he said, the same pitiless self-cross-examination continued. He could not avoid those incidents which raised it, and yet could not mistake in the faces of his listeners their sense that his account was incomplete.

"We never bunched," he repeated, as though, in describing Heron's visit to the tobacconist's shop, he had had no other purpose than to make clear this small matter of procedure. "If for some reason we had to make our way through a town on foot, we would go if we could at dusk, early or late, but not so late or so early that there weren't plenty of people about; we needed them for cover; nothing was less safe than for us to clank alone through dark, empty streets. Our method was what we called a chain.

"I remember one evening, when the time came for us to leave a town where we had been lying up, our Nurse — she was the widow of a watchmaker, under forty, but grey; plump once but had run to loose flesh; a bleak, lonely, bitter woman who worked for the River Line in white hatred of the enemy and cared for nothing on earth except the birds she kept in cages — she said that at an exact hour, in a side-street to the north of the market-square, a covered van would be waiting. It was going twenty miles into the country to pick up a German working-party and bring them in. It had all the permits and would get out easily. At eighteen miles, it would drop us in a wood. From that point onwards we had our instructions; we should find our new shelter before night. The difficulty was to get us to the van. The driver, though he would take us if we came to him, wouldn't venture off his customary route to come to us. We were well to the south of the market-square. We had to reach it, cross it and find our way beyond it. The watch-maker's wife led the chain; Heron followed; I came next; Frewer last. If Heron lost sight of her, or I of him, or Frewer of me, we were lost. No going forward; she alone knew that van-driver. No going back — anyhow not for hours; she lived alone with her birds, and the place was locked.

"The rules of the chain were: keep the longest possible intervals, and don't look back: never look back to see if the other fellow is following. My part was probably the easiest; Heron was tall, I could watch his head; but it was bad enough. At corners or in a crowd-bunch, you were bound to lose sight sometimes, and then you had to hold yourself in, not to quicken pace, not to lose the interval, not — well, not to panic and give the man behind no chance. Half a dozen times I lost sight of Heron, and said to myself: now it has happened! now what do I do? and my mind began to dart hither and thither trying to decide whether to fall back on Frewer or whether to go on blind and try to strike down into the market-square independently or . . . Anyhow, pretty near panic half a dozen times; and then I would catch sight of Heron again, and grin like a dog and spread my toes out inside my boots and sweat with relief."

They had finished supper and he saw his hand shake as he lifted his chair away from the table.

"Shall we go out?" Mrs. Muriven said, but he wanted to stay indoors; at that instant he wanted the enclosure of friendly walls, and he said: "May we a little later?"

"Of course. We will have coffee here."

He sat in silence, watching the flame wrap its tongues round the glass bowl.

" But you kept your interval," Valerie said. Her saying this touched him. It supplied a need and gave him confidence as though her hand had steadied his; but he did not wish to take credit to himself for what others had done equally. " We all did," he answered. " You may lose your head, and let every sort of shivering panic make cowards of your arms and legs and spine, but if there *is* a rule not to look back, not to increase pace suddenly, the chain does hold. Anyhow it held me. . . . I'm not sure that Heron needed it," he added with surprise at his own thought. " In really tight corners, he had a kind of amused, salty calm as if for two pins he'd make himself invisible and just glide out of it. And this time something happened for which the rules of the chain didn't provide."

He fell into a silence from the midst of which he saw the ladies watching him. " In a long street," he continued, speaking now as casually as he could, " when I thought all was plain sailing, and I could see not only Heron but the watchmaker's wife well ahead, I found I was closing on him; then grasped that he had stopped. Something in German uniform — a corporal, it turned out — had him, as I first saw it, by the hand; what I couldn't see then was that Heron's hand was held out knuckles upward; the German, who had asked him the time, was peering at his wrist-watch before setting his own by it. So Heron told me afterwards. I wasn't to know that at the time. All I knew was that, whether the encounter was friendly or unfriendly, Heron was losing distance. In two minutes, he'd lose our Nurse and the snake would be without a head. I dared not stop. There was nothing to do but go on, increase pace a little but not enough to spoil Frewer's game, pass Heron if necessary — above all, keep the watchmaker's wife in sight. Gradually I came up with Heron. He was talking and laughing with the man; his back was to me, he didn't know I was near; and just as I was within reach — I could have touched him by stretching out a hand — just at that moment . . ." Sturgess felt a thickness rise in his throat, but he managed to jerk out: ". . . they parted."

The omission had been so obvious that for a moment he expected his listeners to cry out against it and was bewildered by their silence. If they had cried out, he might have been able to say that, at the moment before separation, Heron had leaned down to the level of the corporal and spoken in his ear, and that the corporal's expression had seemed receptive and knowing — the expression of a man to whom some confidence or message or order had been given; or the expression, perhaps, of a man who had had a satisfying joke whispered into his ear. Which? Sturgess had not known which, and did not now. The corporal had smiled, but with a pushing up of his underlip on one side of his mouth.

18

Before supper, he had said to Valerie, of herself and Heron, that he was " beginning to know " them both, and now his words came back to him with a fresh impact of truth. In the garden, where they sat at the water's edge looking up towards the bridge and the appearing lights of the village, he began to describe the Chassaignes' house and their arrival there. He felt, as he did so, not that he was telling, but that he was being told, a story, that he didn't know the end of it and had yet to discover, like a new arrival, the life at the Chassaignes' and the part that Heron would play in it.

They were put down at night at the side of a straight, empty, treeless road. Their driver did not stop his engine but drove away at once. Parallel with the road, at a few yards' distance, was a ditch or trench, deep enough for them to stand in without exposing their heads. In this they stood and waited as they had been ordered. Heron was tall enough to look out, but the night was dark, he reported nothing, and the woman who came for them appeared unexpectedly in their trench, not having approached it by the road. She spoke a pass-word ; each of them in turn replied as he had been told to reply ; she said : " *Suivez*," and they followed her by a sunken track and a long copse into a field, which they did not cross but skirted.

They came then into a yard or walled garden. A stream was audible ahead as they turned into the house.

When their guide, without hesitation in the darkness, lighted a candle and held it up to look at them, a square, stone-flagged room appeared with a narrow gallery on two sides of it and steps at the corner. She said in English: "You are welcome, gentlemen. . . . Will you move quietly please? It is not that you are not safe. It is only that we pass through my father's room. He is old. We try not to disturb him." With that she turned and they followed.

They had not far to go. The house was small, but its ways were tortuous, the passages narrow and broken by little flights of two or three steps, up or down. Having climbed to the gallery and passed round in single file, they came, by three short passages, of which the last seemed to turn back upon the first, into what appeared to be a wing of the house but was, in fact, the oldest part of it, to which the rest had long ago been added. Here they entered a room in which, upon a narrow bed, his head raised on high, hard pillows, an old man, with a full white moustache clipped to a straight line above his lips, was lying on his back. His daughter shaded her candle, but needlessly, for he was awake with wide, staring eyes.

" I am awake," he said.

" Father, you ought not to be awake. You must sleep on in the morning."

" I shall do nothing of the kind. My mind works in the morning. . . . Now leave us, Marie. I will tell these gentlemen what to do."

His reason, they were to understand afterwards, was that he wished to tell them that the second door of his room, at the foot of his bed, opened into a closet where each night and morning they might empty their slops and draw water from a tap. This he would not allow his daughter to speak of. If he could give her no other protection in a maddened world, he could to this extent protect her modesty.

"Very well," she answered, "then I will say good-night. I have only certain provisional orders to give. The rest can wait until the morning. Which is the senior officer among you?"

"I am the senior," Heron said.

She looked at him carefully, assessing the man with whom she had to deal. Then, swinging her candle, she showed him a ladder running up to a door. "The room above," she said, "was once a granary; then when I was a child a kind of playroom or workroom for me — I used to live there when I wasn't at school. Now it is a lumber-room, half full of shelves and books and much else. It has no other entrance from the house than this, but it has a double granary door which leads on to an outside platform and a ladder to the ground. The granary door was blocked up. We have unsealed it for emergency. But no one in Blaise has seen it open since I was a child. Except in extreme emergency, it must not be opened. That is the first order."

"I understand," Heron replied.

"My father, as you see," she said, "has a stove. As the pipe goes up, the granary stove-pipe joins it. My father works as well as sleeps in this room. Now and then he receives Germans here. We think it wise."

"*She* thinks it wise," the old man said.

"It is interesting," Heron answered. "I think it very wise, I understand perfectly."

"For that reason," Marie continued, "there are two further rules. First, if the stove-pipe is tapped——"

"Does it sound unmistakably?" Heron put in.

She smiled then for the first time. "It was a nursery legend," she said. "It sounds like a suit of armour falling down. . . . If it is tapped, it means that Father has a visitor — French or German makes no odds, we trust no one — and you neither move nor speak until you are told that you may. That is the second order."

"And the third?"

"If the signal is given again, it will mean that a visitor is coming up to your room. You open the granary doors, go on to the platform, close them, descend. Is it understood?"

"Perfectly. . . . We should be seen?"

"Only the platform is visible from the road. Once down, you will not be seen unless there are enemy in the courtyard itself. You will see a pile of wood against the courtyard wall. Scale the wall, drop, turn right, and follow the ditch until, at a hundred metres, it is crossed by a little footbridge. At that point, the bridge is overgrown by thicket. Lie and wait. If I never come, move by stages to Virac-St.-Just. Report to Charlotte, a grocer's shop, rue Fourès twelve. The word to her is 'Pyramides'. To-morrow I will repeat this and give you more detail. . . . One thing more. To-night you must go to bed without lights. A light may show. There is a part of the room in which you may have light safely. To-morrow I will show you. Until then——"

She was about to go when Frewer said: "Could you tell us, mademoiselle, how long we are likely to stay here?"

After considering him attentively, she asked: "You are eager to be gone?"

"Oh no, it isn't that," he explained hastily, embarrassed by the thought that he might have seemed discourteous to a hostess. "It isn't that at all. It's just a question of what gear we go into."

This was not at once within the reach even of her English. "Into what gear?"

" I mean: whether we come out of top gear, whether we settle."

" There is a possibility that you may go forward to-morrow night. If not, you may be here a long time."

Frewer didn't answer, but smiled like a tired boy.

" You can be comfortable and safe," she said. " You can be at peace. Unless there should be a visitor in this room, you need not moderate your voices. You can talk and move freely."

" Has any visitor," Heron asked, " ever shown any desire to come up ? "

" No," she said, " none. The ladder is always there as an invitation. A German is too clever to do anything that he is invited to do." Then suddenly she asked: " You come from Germany ? "

" Yes, mademoiselle."

" The others from the air ? "

" I see you know all our case-histories."

" Ah well, yes," she said, " it is necessary to know the contents of one's parcels before they come."

She went over to her father, knelt beside his bed, kissed him, and asked whether he had written well that day.

" Very little," he replied.

" But well ? And happily ? "

" Happily," he answered.

" About what ? "

" A leaf. Set deep in the midst of foliage, in the dark, as the soul is. Every movement, you understand, the shifting of a bird, the turn of a breeze, is the opportunity of light to enter, of the leaf to be touched by it. And the leaf feels the light flow up its edge and recede like a tide, but, for all that day, no more; and night comes, and the cool night air like the touch of your forehead on my cheek, and with it the solitude of the leaf." He looked up across her shoulder. " Our guests are waiting, my dear. They, too, are like little children waiting to be asked whether they have written well to-day. I am foolish and deep in hatred, but my leaf does not hate or fear. Will you sharpen my pencils before you go ? "

19

THE room in which they awoke next morning had, in Sturgess's recollection, a quality of peace that he did his utmost to communicate, and he thought, as he watched Valerie's face, that he had succeeded at least so far as to make her an inhabitant of the room. " It was a peaceful room," he said at first, but the word " peaceful " had been so often used that it conveyed, he knew, little of what he intended — nothing, perhaps, of what was positive in his sensation of the room; and he went on to say that the room was " good ", that it was " untroubled ", and, finally, that he had felt it to be a harbour from which one might penetrate inland into—

" Into what ? " Mrs. Muriven asked.

He answered, quite shamelessly: " Into the Golden World."

Valerie lifted her head and caught her breath. " That was sudden, too ! "

" Does it mean anything — anything seizable, I mean ?" he asked. " Or are they just round, romantic words ? "

" No," she answered. " The Golden World is the core of every tragedy. Otherwise it wouldn't be tragedy — only hurt and waste and dreariness."

The quality that he had discovered in the room was the harder to communicate because he was bound to say, when he came to describe it, that it had no windows.

" A playroom without windows ! " Mrs. Muriven exclaimed at once.

"Ah, but in its playroom days the granary door could be opened, and that," he said, "was like opening a wall. . . . But that isn't the point," he added hastily. "I shall never make you understand what the room was if I try to explain away the fact that it was windowless and yet was not blind."

The light, he told them, came from a double skylight in a beamed, shadowy roof. It was this that he noticed on waking: the shafts of daylight, the roof-beams and the bookshelves standing out in mid-floor filled him with a sense of depth and tranquillity. "You know," he said, "how, when you have fever, everything becomes a thousand thousand times larger — or smaller — than life, everything swells or shrinks; it seems to be breathing in terror, and you rise and fall with its exaggerated breath. I felt, as I stared at the room, the converse of that: there were no fevers; it was as if I were looking at a child sleeping, or a solitary tree, or a wild mountain; everything was natural and calm."

He paused then, for in his mind he was looking at Heron's sleeping head as he had looked at it that morning without admixture of doubt, without entanglement of circumstance: the head, as he saw it then, of one innocent and admirable.

"After a little while," he said, "Heron woke; then Frewer. Heron awoke like no one else I have ever seen. He came out of sleep without any shock or hesitation, but completely. At one moment he was sound asleep, with long, quiet breath; the next he was sitting up in full possession of himself. We found basins and a jug of water. We washed, and shaved, put on such clothes as we had taken off, and soon Marie brought us breakfast. We had a chance to see her then, but scarcely to talk. She must go to her *lycée*; meanwhile there were orders to give. She said that the room must never have the appearance of being inhabited. Our mattresses must be rolled up; our crockery kept together on its tray, able to be disposed of instantly in a niche reserved for it among other crockery piled on a dresser against the west wall; our own small belongings must be packed away, not in recognizable piles, but dispersedly, each in its separate place among the entangled lumber of that huge room. There were chairs and a table, pictures hanging and pictures piled against chair-legs, rugs on the floor, recognizable signs of the room's having once been an inhabited schoolroom; these might remain, and, in emergency, be abandoned as they were; 'and if you read a book,' she said, 'have the table and the floor near you piled with a vast untidiness of books into which your book can be dropped like a cupful of water into the ocean. Untidiness is the salvation of this place. Put nothing in order, except your own plans. . . . The emergency won't arise,' she added. 'There was once a formal search of the whole house, but they were very correct, they took nothing. Since then—' She shrugged her shoulders. 'We invite them to come so far, into my father's room, and we have such warning of their coming along the gallery, through the house, that this room is as safe as any in France. The emergency will not arise. Probably, in all the time you are here, no one will come even into my father's room. But you will prepare.' She looked at Heron. 'You will plan every movement and rehearse it continually. Is that understood? . . . In the top shelf of that toy-cupboard you will find a grimy pack of cards. Play with it, but never on the table; only on the floor, the bare floor with the rug thrown back. In emergency, one of you — decide which — puts into his pocket the cards that happen to be in his hand. Then the rug comes over. If it should be turned back again, what is found there is the incomplete debris of a long-forgotten game. Is that also understood? The object is that you shall be able, soundlessly and within sixty seconds, to walk through those granary doors and—' " Sturgess sat up straight in his chair, a hand on each knee, as though he were listening. " I remember her exact words, and how, as she said them, she looked at us with longing as though we were ghosts who would vanish, and at Heron with sadness and wonder. She spoke lightly, but the words went through me. ' The object is,' she said, ' that you shall be able, soundlessly and within sixty seconds, to walk through those granary doors and leave not a rack behind.' She looked at us again in a way that brought home to me suddenly the loneliness of her own peril. We were at least in company; our adventure had an end to look forward to. Hers, none. When we were gone, more ghosts would come from nowhere, and be men for a little while, and pass on, and be ghosts again. Then more, without end. But she was undaunted. ' Now I must go and teach my other pupils,' she said.

" Heron asked what was the routine of the house while she was away. She told us briefly as much as immediately affected us. Her father, who had risen at five, would work until noon. No one else would be in the house. A woman came in to work sometimes but only when Marie was there to work with her. If a visitor knocked, her father would give the first signal and himself go to the door. In any case, we were not to go down into his room during his working hours. At noon she would come back and see us again for a few moments. In the evening, when her work at the *lycée* was done, she would talk further. Meanwhile, she said, there were many books and a little food, and — with a glance at Heron — the plan for emergency to be worked out in detail and rehearsed.

"We worked it out. We worked it out for every conceivable circumstance — eating, reading, playing cards: not sleeping, for we should never, all three, be asleep at once; we should divide the nights into three watches, and the first signal would have us all awake. That first day, we rehearsed pretty continuously, and at night so that we could act in the dark. Heron drove us like a drill-sergeant or a ballet-master. Every movement of hand or foot was planned — 'sixty seconds and soundlessly' — we could quit that room without a trace. The drill became part of our routine. Without warning, twice, three times a day, sometimes when Marie herself was with us, Heron gave the word 'sixty seconds' and we did instantly what we had to do up to the point of lifting the bar of the granary door. . . . A waste of time as it turned out. No visitors came while we were at Blaise."

20

STURGESS's memory of the time he spent in the Chassaignes' granary did not divide itself into an orderly succession of days, nor did the account he gave of it to Mrs. Muriven and Valerie. He thought of it as a single experience bracketed in his life, appearing differently to him whenever he considered it, but nevertheless single, as a book is single and not a succession of chapters, or as a jewel is single as it lies in the palm of your hand, though its facets move and its fires change.

As soon as they knew from Marie that the possibility of their going forward on the second day was past and that they were to wait indefinitely, perhaps for ten days, perhaps for much longer, Sturgess asked whether it was for anything in particular that they were waiting. She said: "Yes," and no more.

"For something else than the ordinary arrangements of transport?"

"Yes," she said, "but you mustn't cross-examine me."

"But there is one thing, mademoiselle, that I should like to ask," Frewer said, rubbing the side of his face and pulling down the lid of his right eye with a nervous, clutching movement of his fingers. "May I ask it? It would make a lot of difference to me if I might."

"Yes," she said, "of course you may ask."

"It is this. Am I right in thinking that, until something definite has happened — something, I mean, that we shall recognize as having happened inside this room — that, until then, we don't go forward ? "

" Yes," she said.

" The thing we are waiting for — I don't ask what it is — whatever it is, we shall know it when it comes ? "

" Yes," she answered.

Sturgess had not known what Frewer was driving at; nor, perhaps, had she. But Heron had known.

" You can come out of top gear, Dick. You can go to sleep. . . . Go to sleep now."

" Shall I ? Yes, I think I will. I have eight hours. It's my morning watch. Call me at four." He heaved himself up in his armchair. " Don't let me disturb you. I'll go and curl up." But he did not rise. " A great deal of travelling always did tire me, even when I was a boy."

He gave himself a comfortable twist in his chair, his head fell over sideways, and he was asleep.

Marie's eyebrows moved.

" No," Heron said, " he's all right. He'll stick it."

Sturgess suggested that the boy would sleep better on his mattress, but Heron wouldn't have it.

" Let him have his own way. If he wakes, he'll like to see us here. If he goes really deep, I'll carry him through without waking him. We'll split his morning watch, Philip. Let him sleep the clock round if he can."

They were sitting in the part of the granary which they called the Sardine Box or, later, the Box. It was, in effect, an irregular, four-sided room, measuring some five paces on its longest diagonal. Two of its sides were walls, running into a corner where the granary roof sloped to within four feet of floor level; a third side was the back of a huge glass-fronted bookcase, hoisted in through the granary doors long ago, and pushed back into the corner as far as the angle of the roof would allow; and the fourth side, hoisted into place when daylight failed, was an old curtain tacked to a roof-beam and tacked so lightly that, in emergency, it could be instantly pulled down. Here, with the fourth wall folded back, there was light enough by day, and here, in the dark hours, they could use a lantern without fear that a door-chink or the glow of imperfectly shrouded skylights would show that the granary was inhabited. Heron loved the place. By him they were drawn into using it more than they might otherwise have done, and at times when there was no need for the concealment of lights. There was one armchair in it, that in which Frewer had fallen asleep: no other furniture, lest the Box should ever have the appearance of a room lived in. The floor, with rug rolled or spread, was their table and, with the low corner-walls, their chairs. There they would sit, sometimes side by side, to share a lantern on the ground between them, sometimes divided by the corner, their feet converging; and there, leaning against a wall, the roof-beams springing out above her, Marie, when she was not at work or with her father, would often sit with them in talk or silence, coming at first, Sturgess thought, to observe them and be sure that her orders were obeyed, then for the assuagement of solitude and secrecy that their company gave her, then —

He broke away from his narrative, seeking the word. "To be with Heron," he said at last.

"You mean," said Mrs. Muriven with her habitual plunge for the concrete, the defined, "that she fell in love with him?"

Sturgess smiled. "Since you put it so, I think, in fact, she did, though it wasn't, I'm sure, a thing acknowledged by her then; her discipline, and his, ruled it out, and, I suppose, the utter hopelessness of it, placed as we were. . . . In any case," he added, " though it may have been, in a sense, true, that isn't what I meant. I meant just what I said: ' to be with Heron '."

" To be with him ? " Valerie repeated.

" We all felt it. Frewer and I, just as much as Marie."

Mrs. Muriven again reached out for a clearly marked label to stick on a pigeon-hole in her mind. " You mean," she said, " that you felt him to be what is called a ' leader of men ' ? "

Sturgess shook his head. " I doubt whether he was. He led us because the circumstances happened to require it of him. . . . No," Sturgess continued, " it wasn't that." Then, with a swift smile and a tilt of his head, he demanded of Valerie: " Do you happen to know the meaning of the word ' serene ' ? "

" Doesn't it mean ' calm, unruffled ' ? "

" It means also ' clear, translucent, with light shining through '."

" I see," she said.

" Do you ? That was Heron's quality. Not just calm. Not just cheerful or optimistic — he wasn't, particularly, either of these. I suppose that what Mrs. Muriven speaks of as a ' leader ' is generally a man who gives an impression of being in himself a source of power. Heron didn't give that impression. However dark or confused the *expression* of the world was, you felt, with him, that there was an interior light, and you were happy because you were sure of that, not in the least because you believed that the cruelty of outward experience would greatly change or that there was ' a good time coming '. . . . Poor Frewer didn't believe there was a good time coming for him. That evening, I remember, when, after a little while, it had been decided to carry him to bed, Heron, standing beside Frewer's chair and watching him sleep, asked me: 'Has he ever told you what his "war aims" are?' When I shook my head, he went on: 'He told me. All the talk about isms and ologies doesn't mean any more to him than it did to — well, to Nelson. He has one perfectly clear idea, all in one word: England.' . . . Heron looked at us to see whether we took that straight; then stooped, picked the boy up, said three words to quiet him when he stirred, and carried him off.

"When he returned he sat down in his old place with his back to the wall. 'Dick knows,' he said, 'that, when he gets into the air again, he's going to be killed.' . . . 'Knows?' I asked. . . . 'Oh yes,' Heron answered without a trace of scepticism, 'sometimes men know. He does, certainly.' This astonished me. Frewer was tired out, I knew, and during the last few days had acquired certain nervous habits — the pulling down of his eyelid was one; but that was only physical and temporary, rest would cure it; by and large, he was completely unruffled, very silent, very polite and conventional on the surface, very friendly below it; happy, I felt sure, in the unexpressive way in which some Englishmen are happy — anyhow not at all what I imagined a boy would be who was obsessed by a fear that he was going to be killed. When I said this, Heron mocked at my phrase. 'Dick,' he said, 'isn't in the least obsessed by fear. The thing worried him at first. It made him want *not* to get to England, and yet, at the same time, he wanted this journey of ours to end. That was a split, and it worried him. It doesn't now.' . . . 'Why?' I asked. . . . 'Well,' Heron answered, 'if you asked him, he'd say, as he hasn't many words, that after all a chap can only die once; but what it really comes to is that he has passed through the idea, which used to frighten him, that death is either a going into solitude and cold and darkness or a going forward into the unknown. He has begun to see it as a recall — back from this world with its few friends and its millions of insane strangers and its clashing darkness — back from that to a light and sanity which isn't solitary or cold or unknown but was familiar to him in childhood and is familiar now whenever he looks at a tree or a sky or a mountain or a human being, and for a moment the nature of things shines through their appearances. The *feel* of that comes to different people in different ways,' Heron continued. 'Dick Frewer told me once, quite suddenly and *à propos* of nothing, that when he was a small boy he used to sit up in his cot chanting *The Ancient Mariner* at the top of his voice. His point was that he hadn't done it for the poem's meaning, or, really, for its sound, which, as he said, must have been pretty hideous. He had done it, he told me, because that particular poem let him get back through it into a world where he belonged and where there was nothing he was afraid of or didn't understand. He has come to see death in the same way.' . . . 'As you do?' Marie asked. . . . 'Yes,' said Heron, 'because, except in blind moments which are pretty frequent, I see life in that way. Our experiences here are centrifugal; they grow away from the centre, as leaves or flowers grow away from the earth; but the earth remains; the centre, the unity, the origin of all experience remains, and life recalls us to it away from —' he made an indrawing circular movement of his hand — 'away from all this circumference of mess and glory. Isn't it what your father was talking about that night when we arrived? That leaf in his poem, deep in the darkness of a tree with light from outside lapping up over its edge sometimes, and then darkness coming over it again, is our life as we ordinarily live it; but your father's leaf was aware of an undivided world where, in its essence, it belonged; and your father's poems, as I understand them, all aim at being — what? — filaments through which the charge from *that* life flows into *this* experience. Isn't that true?' 'They are very unlike *The Ancient Mariner*,' Marie said. 'They are intellectually hard.' . . . 'That may be,' Heron answered, 'but the charge and the light and the magnetism find their own channels. Intellect is one. And anyway,' he added with a smile, 'are you denying intellect to Coleridge?'

"While they talked of Pierre Chassaigne's poetry," Sturgess said, "I watched Heron and I thought of Dick Frewer, asleep on his mattress in the other part of the room; and I grasped what it was that Heron had given to Frewer, and gave to me too. In the first place, intimacy. That silent boy had, pretty obviously, poured his heart out to Heron; so had I in a different way. I don't know how to put it except by saying that one *opened* to the light and warmth of him. He had faults — plenty of them, anyhow from my point of view. Though he was wonderfully gentle to anyone seen separately, he was too little of a humanitarian for me. I mean, he had precious little generalized sympathy with any *group* of people — any race or class or generation — who complained that life hadn't given them a square deal. Life, for him, was what you made it. You took your chance and you took the consequences. If you grumbled against fate or in a generalized way against war, he had no patience with you; it was for him as futile as grumbling about the weather. Often to me he seemed to make too little distinction between men and the rest of nature; he thought of all our attempts to organize collectively as being of value on an administrative level but as powerless to change the governing factors of existence: on that level, they cancelled out, raising one class to lower another, softening one kind of cruelty to harden another, increasing quantities to debase quality, always roughly cancelling out.

"That, if you apply it to modern democracies, is a long way from my own way of thinking; but it gave to Heron an extraordinary steadfastness in his personal life — the kind of reassuring steadfastness that deep countrymen have sometimes who can't be dismayed or made frantic by men's failures to avert disaster, partly because they don't expect men to produce a new heaven and a new earth, and partly because their reckoning of disaster is completely different from ours. To them we aren't the lords of creation who could produce a utopia if only we were clever enough. To them — and to Heron, I think — we are much more like the leaves of a tree, and leaves don't hold a parliament to legislate against the winds or to postpone the autumn, and then blame the other leaves when the gale comes. That was his point of view; it would have disqualified him as a modern statesman," said Sturgess almost wistfully as though he were unsure whether this was praise or blame, "but it gave him roots. When I was rattled and arid, when I felt quite simply that civilization had gone mad like a railroad system without signals that was piling up on its own debris, I found him as comforting as a tree, single and firm, drawing up sap from the earth. He was that to me when I tried to face life, and that, I suppose, is what he was to Dick Frewer, aged twenty, trying to face death."

Sturgess turned to Mrs. Muriven. "You are quite right. Marie loved him. But her father didn't. He was fascinated, he preferred Heron's company to ours, and I thought at first he valued Heron as we did, but was in some way shy of him. But I was wrong. He valued him

— and almost hated him." Sturgess was silent, looking away up the lawn, then at the lowered glint of the river, before he could bring himself to say without too much emphasis: "Chassaigne valued him as one values an enemy."

21.

THE emphasis that Sturgess had so carefully avoided was supplied by Mrs. Muriven's almost indignant question: " An enemy? Why on earth should Pierre Chassaigne have regarded Heron as an enemy?"

Sturgess retreated from the word, murmuring that it had perhaps been too strong. " Still," he said, " there was, from the very beginning, a kind of distrustful watchfulness. I became aware of it one afternoon on which Heron and I had been sitting with Chassaigne — I saying very little because they were discussing German poetry, which was beyond me. It was an animated and, I thought, a very friendly discussion; the old man was learned and precise; he pulled his chair up close to Heron's, opened the book they were arguing about and laid it out between them — on both their knees, so to speak, and ran a long finger-nail under the lines that proved his point. All that struck me then was the uncomfortable physical closeness of the position he chose and the almost querulous eagerness with which he probed Heron's knowledge of German literature. Heron said what he had said before to us — that he had German relations and that the language was as natural to him as English; but he never chattered about his own background and, in the end, Chassaigne stopped pressing him, and muttered that it was remarkable, altogether remarkable, which sounded to me like a compliment. Heron took it so and fended it off by saying that the old man's knowledge of German literature went much deeper than his. . . . 'Ah well,' said Chassaigne, 'so it ought. I professed it once. But I speak German with a French accent.' . . . 'I believe you do that on purpose!' Heron exclaimed, and Chassaigne chuckled; it was the kind of jest that appealed to his intransigence.

"All seemed to be well after that, but, when we were going away and Heron had climbed up the ladder and I was still at the bottom of it, Chassaigne beckoned me back — there was an engraving of old New York that he thought would interest me — and there and then began to question me about Heron's background. There was little I could tell him. It was surprising how little I did know, seeing how much I had told Heron of myself; and yet," he added reflectively, "not necessarily surprising, perhaps; we are all so well satisfied to talk about ourselves that a man who is a natural listener, as Heron was, seems, when our attention is drawn to it as mine was by Chassaigne, to have been almost . . . deliberately . . . reticent.

"This, certainly, was in Chassaigne's mind. . . . 'I once knew a man like that,' he said. 'He was — or I thought he was — an intimate friend, my nearest friend for almost two years. And then something happened — never mind what; to do with women, of course, and money too; it always is, isn't it, money and women; we were young in those days; and not only money and women, but honour too, honour too . . . now what was I saying?' . . . The old man was yellow with wrath and confusion. His lower lip was pushed out and he was blowing upward into the forest of his moustache. He who never failed to control a sentence, phrase by phrase, to the end, had completely lost track of this, and, to cover his lapse, he leant forward in his chair and began to tug at his boot-laces and glance at me over his shoulder with his forehead puckered into wrinkles and a pathetic, pursued look. Then he sat up and made himself smile. . . . ' Ah yes, as I was saying, then something happened — no matter what, a betrayal, you might say — which made me look back over those two years, and grasp that I knew nothing of my friend, nothing. It was my door that had always stood open; his had always *seemed* to be ajar, but he had never let me in. There are people like that: the modest, reticent ones. . . .' Chassaigne was idly turning the page of the quarto that contained engravings of old New York — always the same page, backwards and forwards — and I thought the spasm was over, but it wasn't. He had a blue river-scene by Sisley hanging on his wall — Marie has it at Stanning now — and he walked over to it, and stared at it, and blinked, and burst out: ' My friend's name was Weitbrecht. It was at Leipzig. He was very tall and dark.' . . . The spasm was over then. He closed the book and began to roll his head gently from side to side as if he were dandling a child. . . . ' But there, there, what does it matter? Why do I disturb myself with old memories? That was at the beginning of the century, forty years ago and more.' "

To Sturgess, as he told this, it had seemed that he was giving an honest and complete account of the incident. What it came to was that some association, in Chassaigne's mind, between Heron and a faithless friend tormentingly remembered, some freakish resemblance of appearance or manner, had stirred in him an irrational distrust. Mrs. Muriven accepted this. " Of course," she said, " it all linked up with Chassaigne's hatred of Germans; the man Weitbrecht was for him a symbol." It often happened, she continued, that our liking or disliking of a person met for the first time depended upon some irrelevant hint from the past, and she gave instances.

While she did so Sturgess was remembering that, when the scene with Chassaigne was over and he had climbed back into the granary, he hadn't at first wanted to meet Heron's eyes. "What's the matter with you, Philip?" Heron had said. "You looked then, for a moment, as though you had seen a snake." . . . His impulse had been to warn Heron; to give, at any rate, some casual indication that the old man had taken a dislike to him. But he said nothing. His own mind had been confused. Whatever he had said at that moment, with the taste of Chassaigne's distrust in his mouth, would have been, not precisely false, but inaccurate, and he had shied away, he had spoken indifferently of other things.

That evening, when Marie brought them their supper, he had asked her whether the name Weitbrecht had any special meaning for her. Why? she had said. Has Father been speaking of Weitbrecht to you? I know very little except that he was a friend who became an enemy. . . . Is he alive? Sturgess had asked. . . . Alive? Good heavens no! He was killed long ago in the attack on Verdun. He isn't a subject of conversation to be encouraged. It disturbs Father's work. . . . She had spoken distractedly, scarcely attending to Sturgess's questions. He might have asked more, had it not been evident that her mind was elsewhere. She had sat in uneasy silence while they ate. Twice she had looked at her watch, and the second time had firmly covered its face by clasping her right hand over it, as if she were saying to herself: don't be a fool, don't keep on looking at your watch. Then with a sigh that was not in her character as they had hitherto known it, she had told them that they were to expect a new arrival that night. They were to prepare a place for him to sleep, and to stay awake to receive him. Soon after midnight, I shall go out to find him, she said. If things go as they should, I ought to be back by one-ten or a little sooner. But he's alone; he is finding his own way to the meeting-place. There may be delays.

" She looked," Sturgess said, as he recounted this, " narrow and grey. She seemed to have shrunk, like a young, tired cat. She was sitting on the floor with her feet drawn up under her, and she stared at the room as if she didn't want to leave it; then her eyes rested on Heron; she was thinking that she might be seeing him for the last time."

No sooner had he said this than Sturgess began to wonder whether he was sentimentalizing that slow regard. Always there must have been in her mind — he saw that now, in long retrospect — always, when she looked at Heron, there must have been the clear knowledge that the report on him, which she had received from Brussels, gave him by no means a clear bill. It was her duty to watch him; even to suspect him — to be open continually to any evidence against him.

" When she looked at him with that expression of possible farewell," Sturgess continued, " Heron seemed not to notice its application to him personally; he was never on the look-out for things to flatter him; it surprised him to be loved. But he wasn't blind to other people's suffering. He hadn't missed that she was on edge that night and, to our astonishment, he said: ' I am coming with you.' She flinched as though he had put his arm round her. The expression that passed over her face then was the deepest mingling of delight and agony. She accepted and rejected his offer in the same instant. I saw the rejection as well as the acceptance; I could, I wasn't affected; but Heron couldn't; in that split second he was blind except to what he wanted to see.

The flash of acceptance, of rapturous submission to his will, the desire to put aside her sole responsibility and to share it with him, the aching desire to have him with her — that was what he saw, I suppose. At that moment the artificial rules which governed our relationship with her snapped for him. He would take command, and thought he might. He stood up. 'No,' she said, scarcely audibly. He remained standing; he didn't argue, he assumed that he could overrule her. Even when she told him to sit down, he didn't take it. Then, unmistakably as an order, she repeated it. He obeyed, sat down, said nothing. That was all.

"That night Wyburton came. He had been dropped into France as an agent, had been there eight weeks. This was his way home again, other ways having failed, and the River Line had been told to wait for him. Next morning Frewer asked if this was what we had been waiting for. She said it was. 'So now,' Frewer said, 'we go into top gear again?' 'Not yet,' Marie answered.

"Arrangements for our transport on our last stage, straight through to the Spanish frontier, had been thrown out by the delay. They had to be tied up again; it would take time. The trouble was, Marie told us, that now, when the machine turned over again, it would have to turn over simultaneously all along the line, to release the hold-up. There were others farther back who would have to move into our places on the night after we went, and others behind them. There was no margin for a hitch. Once the day and the hour were fixed, we must go forward at all costs. She hated that and feared it. There were nights sometimes when she knew it wasn't safe to move. Once she had let the transport go empty and waited for a better night. Only once; it wasn't to be done often; but the option was necessary in an extreme emergency. 'Now I shall have no choice,' she said. 'The time-table will be inflexible.' "

The last words she had repeated in French, and they had so engraved themselves on Sturgess's memory that he also repeated them in French. The inflexibility of the time-table had been, in great part, responsible for the violent ending of their days in the granary; it had left no time for questioning, had forced his hand, and hers, and Wyburton's; it had screwed up all the indecisions of his mind into a tight knot demanding to be cut instantly, and now, at the halt of his narrative, he saw that knot tightening, and turned from it.

Mrs. Muriven's voice surprised him. "But it worked?"

He had to drag himself back. "I beg your pardon. What worked?"

"You said the time-table was inflexible . . . but it worked? You got out?"

"Yes."

"Did you ever clear up the small point about the stamps, the envelopes? Did you ask him?"

"No, I didn't ask him."

The question had been a shock. How much had he told Mrs. Muriven? Not of Heron's whispered words to the corporal. Nor of his having bought stamps — presumably because those he had found were too few or had turned out to be unusable. All that Mrs. Muriven had been told was of the click of the desk that night when Heron had shown Frewer his poem. Sturgess wished now that he hadn't told her even this. Why had he allowed her to draw him out? Why had he liked and been flattered by her? He felt angrily that by her discretion, by her skill in not pressing him, she had led him into saying more than he had intended. He determined fiercely to say no more.

A moment later, his respect, if not his liking, for her began to flood back. The fault was not hers. His distress did not spring from what he had told but from what he had avoided. If he had told all that there was to tell, he didn't doubt that she would have approved of the action he had taken. She had that kind of decisive harshness which, though it might justify him now, the warmth of his heart or the niceness of his conscience shrank from. You did what you had to do, he imagined that she might have said. You took your responsibility. Why torment yourself with the consequences? . . . Oh yes, she was, if he would let her be, " on his side " in the trial of himself that persisted in his mind.

But you cannot both kill justly and be innocent of blood, she would have added. You cannot, young man, have it both ways. The world cannot.

It was a dilemma — none other than Hamlet's, he thought — that seemed to him unmodern, medieval, cruel. And yet, Mrs. Muriven would say, it exists. And yet, Heron would have said, it exists.

He looked at Valerie, as though she had been within his mind and would answer him, but she had turned her face away. As he watched her, she stood up and moved a couple of paces towards the landing-stage. He too rose.

" It's getting late," he said, " I must say good-night."

But he was reluctant to go, and they three stood in a compact group, looking down at the water, in desultory, delaying talk. He spoke of Hamlet and noticed that his introduction of the subject seemed to them abrupt and unexplained. The scene in which Hamlet, intending to kill the king, held his hand because the king was praying and because his soul might go to heaven if he died upon his knees, was, he said, the outstanding evidence that Shakespeare was a man of the Renaissance; there was no scene in literature more blackly superstitious; we had outgrown it; it was difficult nowadays to make modern pupils understand what Hamlet's motive had been, or be in any way interested by it.

"Because, you mean, they don't carry their hatreds into the spiritual world?" Valerie asked. "I wonder. Is it hatred they have outgrown or only belief in a spiritual world?"

"I don't think," he answered, "that that is the question as far as they are concerned. Simply on the human plane, the whole dilemma of Hamlet, not in that scene only but throughout the play, the whole dilemma," he repeated, "the choice between a violent action required of him by destiny and the peaceful quietism that was a part of his nature, seems to the modern mind a dilemma that civilization is passing beyond."

"'Passing beyond'?" Valerie asked. "Or 'just beginning to understand'?"

"Anyhow," he answered, "modern people feel that it is a choice which ought not to be forced on rational men."

"'Ought not'?" said Mrs. Muriven. "But it is. It was at Hiroshima, and will be again. The East compels it."

"It tears the conscience," he said. "The Western democracies wish to avoid that tearing."

"Wish . . ." she repeated. "Responsibility is a hard bread to be eaten with a rough wine, not sopped in milk. No one can eat it for us. Eat or starve."

They had turned from the river and crossed the lawn into the house. The little table in the hall, beside which Valerie had been standing when he and Mrs. Muriven had come out of the kitchen earlier in the day, recalled to him the conversation that had followed, and so far away did it seem now that he looked at Valerie inquiringly, as if she were another being, divided from him as an acquaintance is with whom there has never been any intimacy of contact. " I don't understand," she said.

Mrs. Muriven had opened the front door and gone out before them. They could see her through the doorway, her head up, sniffing the air, examining the sky, for evidences of to-morrow's weather.

" What don't you understand ? "

" Anything yet, except that you loved him."

" That may be all that's worth understanding."

" But it makes you unhappy ? "

" He is dead."

" I loved my brother. He is dead. That doesn't — that doesn't *tear* me."

" Leave it," he said.

The abruptness of that appeared to him as a brutality, as if he had struck her, but he could find no gentler words to add. All initiative had ebbed. There was nothing he wanted, at that moment, to do or think or be, neither to stay nor to go, neither to be with her nor to be absent from her. He wanted the past not to have been the past — and seeing the folly and the futility of that wish, he forced himself to be cheerful and politely active, spoke of their meeting to-morrow, said good-night, and swung away towards the lime avenue by which he had come and which would lead him towards the village.

" But you are going the wrong way ! " Mrs. Muriven called.

" The wrong way ? "

" There's no need to go back to the village."

She was advancing towards him and he went to meet her. There was, she said, a path to the left which led up the hillside through the wood and joined the road to the

Wyburtons' within two hundred yards of their gate. It saved more than a mile. "The path Mrs. Wyburton took you by, Valerie, when you went up to borrow the German books."

"I remember it, of course," Valerie said. "It's a good evening. I'll put you on your way."

This, evidently, had been Mrs. Muriven's intention. Neither he nor Valerie would have chosen companionship then.

"Godmother meant well," she said when they were out of earshot.

"She did well," he gallantly and foolishly answered.

What had come between them he did not know. They walked on side by side, unreasoningly afraid of each other. The easy phrases they spoke increased the tension, and they fell into silence, hearing only the soft crackle of the wood-path under their feet.

22

"You said that your brother's death doesn't *tear* you. Why did you use that word?"

"It was yours."

They had been walking in single file on a narrow, ascending path. She stopped and turned, looking down to him from higher ground.

"You said: 'It tears the conscience.' It was your word, Philip."

"Yes, but on another subject."

"I know. But sometimes, though a subject is changed, the old thought goes on."

"You mean—" He looked into her face. "Will you say it? You will say it straighter than I can."

"I have no right to say it."

The barrier between them went down in that instant. "You have the right if you will take it."

"I meant," she then said with that depth and firmness of voice which he had first loved in her, "that your own conscience is torn by your friend's death. Do you know how your face changes when you speak of it, or when——"

"Go on."

"Or when you — when you so terribly avoid speaking of it? . . . Oh, you don't know how your whole being seems to change!" she exclaimed. "It's agony to watch."

"It's strange," he answered, "how everything has altered since I came here — even the past. There's a bit of me, I suppose, that thinks what I want to think. The day before I met you, the whole of that story told itself in my mind as I wanted it to be told. I had selected from it the bits I wanted to remember. But there's an honest bit of me too, and my romantic selection doesn't work any more. The thing comes up out of the past and lives itself; to be with Marie and Julian is to have the stress and the ache of it; and you——"

"I?" she said. "What have I to do with it?"

"More than I can tell."

She smiled, and shook her head.

"Simply to look at you and hear you speak," he continued, "makes what was good in it so near that it is no longer memory, but within reach, as though he really were still alive and I could stretch out my hand and take his . . . as I take yours."

She did not move, but he feared that she might, and said: "Don't take your hand away."

"No."

Instantly, on a flood of impulse and wild confidence, one word: "Never?"

Her fingers tightened; full knowledge of what he had asked shook her.

"My dear, don't ask that now."

"I do ask it."

"Not to-night."

He persisted with a questioning half-breath.

"Because," she replied with that lightening of tone which can give wings to seriousness, "because to-night you are what he used to call 'out of judgment', and so, perhaps, am I."

So be it, but his blood was hot; she near and responding; nevertheless wiser than he; and he trudged on patiently, content that the mood of deadness and flatness, which had seized him in Mrs. Muriven's house and which he despised in his energetic and hopeful self, had passed, and that now he could throw up his head and smell with delight, as though they had been created for him, the resinous and earthy smells of the cooling wood. Above, on their right, this wood was close and continuous; on their left, it would open out now and then into full evening light spread over a steep foreground of lower beech and elm, and a curving valley black-green in the bowl and molten on its farther rim. Above the rim was an area of egg-shell green, from which a series of detached clouds, like the bow-waves of an invisible fleet, wheeled upward, trailing a spindrift of light from their higher edges, and, from their lower, a wake that was slowly dissolved in the horizon's darkening stream.

In one of these wide apertures, they stood to look out. Such an evening may nct come again, Sturgess thought, and sat down, prodigal of time, not looking up but making it a test of fate that he should soon hear the rustle of her coming down and the expectant stillness of her being settled at a little distance from him.

"I think I can tell you," she said, "why my brother's death doesn't 'tear' me; our life together, as far as it went, was so fully lived. I have no regrets for anything wasted or anything hoarded, and I feel that he would have had none. We didn't waste our few years and days and minutes, but neither did we jealously count them over or cling. It was a natural, go-as-you-please relationship, not in the least what is ordinarily called intense. We were often apart and took that in the day's work; we seldom wrote more than scraps of letters, and, if no letter came, that didn't worry us; when we met again, it was never an excited reunion; we picked things up where they were without much telling."

Sturgess listened without moving. Her voice had for

him the faculty of healing, of giving him again by its freshness and young confidence, above all by its manifest affection for him, a renewal of that sense of goodness and sanity in the world, and in his own heart, which was the spring of all his energies. Moreover, in speaking of her brother, and describing incidents of her childhood shared with him and ways of thought learned from him, she was speaking of herself, and Sturgess grasped that he was now learning for the first time small things and great which, if her life and his should ever run together, would be his measure of that distinct past never to be brought by one lover into the full light of experience shared. A picture of her as she had been when she was a very young girl began to shape itself in his imagination as an added reason for loving her now, but he knew well enough that She Then and She Now, though the same in her own consciousness, must always be distinct in his; for even in love, identity could not be passed from one to another. Nevertheless, he felt that, in speaking of her brother, she told more of herself than she knew she was telling or could ever tell by other means, more *to him* at any rate; for the man of whom she spoke began to be, for him, known; and so much of herself was being communicated that he was enthralled. Her love for her brother was, as it were, a cipher by which her own self might be read, and he listened silently, that cipher almost his. Even when her voice ceased, he did not by any word disturb the pause, but waited for her to continue.

"I was thinking of him this evening," she said after a long, untroubled interval, "when Godmother was saying her say — about responsibility being a hard bread that we must eat for ourselves or starve. It is true; but Godmother in some way unbalances it. And I value balance, by which I don't mean just moderation or a willingness to compromise or the old story of on-the-one-hand and on-the-other. I mean what my brother meant when he said: ' lilies of the field '."

This was part of her cipher by which Sturgess was baffled, but he held his peace.

" He used to laugh me out of all sorts of resentments and wild enthusiasms with that phrase," she said thoughtfully. " It didn't at all mean that he took ' no thought for the morrow ' in the sense of being feckless. On the level of conduct, he was as responsible as even Godmother could have wished — a very good officer, although completely without personal ambition. But beyond that level, deeper down, he didn't fret, he had no anxiety of soul. Everything he did, everything even that he thought and felt in the ordinary course of life, was—" She paused for a long time, and Sturgess waited — " was included," she went on. " If I say it was ' included ' like a play, you'll think that I mean he shrugged his shoulders at life — ' all the men and women *merely* players ', with a kind of cynical emphasis on the ' merely '. It wasn't that. There was no ' merely ' about it. No one was ever more burningly aware of the parts other people were playing and of their lives beyond the play. What he meant by ' lilies of the field ' was simply that just as there was a part of him and of everyone that was wrapped up in the happenings of the play and responsible for them, so there was another part independent of them: he wasn't indifferent to the outcome of the play, a good player can't be; but deep down he had, even while playing, an independent life which wasn't and couldn't be affected. So he could accept responsibility without anxiety and — it was you who said that — ' loss without losing '."

" It wasn't I who said it," Sturgess answered, " it was Heron."

On that she made no comment. A bird, wakened by their voices, shook the leaves above them, and the sound, continuing in Sturgess's mind, accented the following stillness. Soon, he thought, we shall get up and walk on, or perhaps, as I know my way, she will return. To-morrow I shall meet her again; we shall go upstream in a boat and picnic on some island — Radlett's Island? — and we shall be in full sunshine, the water will glitter and throw up dapples of light on to the moored boat. The area of her not-knowing will be spread between us. I shall look back upon this moment of my sitting here, and of the owl-echo in the valley, and of Heron's name continuing, the last word spoken, and I shall say: why did you not tell her then? . . . Soon, he thought, his mind circling, we shall get up and walk on. A fear seized him that she was about to move. He turned his eyes and said: " I want you to know . . . and judge."

" My dear," she answered, " tell it as you see it. Not judging yourself. The facts as you see and feel them. How do you know that judgment lies with us? "

23

HE told her the facts as truly and simply as he could.

First, he tried to make it clear that, against his expectation and even now a little to his surprise, Wyburton's coming had not lessened the closeness of the group living in the Chassaignes' granary. "I found him chilly at first," Sturgess said, "chiefly, I suppose, because our set-up, which was still for me a unique adventure, didn't appear so to him. He took it as a bit of routine to which he had to adapt himself in the shortest possible time. As he was new to the River Line, Marie asked him to take the same oath of absolute obedience that I had taken at Brussels. After an instant's pause, he said: 'Yes. Fire away.' She said the words, and he said them after her in a toneless gabble as if they were a formality without meaning. But they had meaning, as you'll see. Afterwards — I mean, long afterwards — I told him that the way he took that oath had shocked me because it had seemed so completely without feeling. 'Feeling?' he said. 'What did you expect? Is a condition of service any more binding because you accept it with a lump in your throat?'

"He had to be fitted in to our established drill for abandoning the granary at the second signal, and he learned quickly and easily, taking orders from Heron. Then, being by rank senior, he revised the drill and improved it. From that time onward, Marie gave her instructions through him. Nothing else was changed —

except," Sturgess added with a certain reluctance, " that our small unit, far from being chilled or divided, was in fact enriched by his being part of it.

" I suppose I'm out of my depth where Julian Wyburton is concerned. I can watch and admire the product of that remarkable machine without knowing — anyhow without feeling — how it works. His link with Heron puzzled me and I'm still not sure that I have it right. It was a Service rather than a human link, and yet not only strong but intimate. Wyburton lived by discipline and secrecy, both carried so far that they had become for him valuable in themselves — or so I say, who, being as the Belgian told me, ' an amateur ', probably don't understand Wyburton at all. I have a moral prejudice against professional militarism which — well, let's leave it that you and Marie, who haven't that prejudice and wouldn't speak of ' militarism ' any way, can probably see much further into Wyburton than I can. On service he's magnificent, instantly and one hundred per cent reliable, quick as a panther and as ruthless——"

" Ruthless ? " Valerie threw in.

" It isn't the right word, I know. Is there another ? "

" Dedicated ? "

" That applies to the service of God."

" Not only."

Well, he thought, to every people its own mysteries; to the British theirs; and, without dispute, he continued: " Off duty I like him, he's genial and kind; but I feel always that nothing off duty is quite real to him any more, and that to me is unnatural. . . . However, my opinion is neither here nor there. The point is that Heron wasn't in the least disturbed. For half a day, he and Wyburton were stiff and guarded with each other; afterwards not at all. They took each other's measure and were satisfied.

Heron's odd gift of drawing men towards him worked again. Within — how do I say that? — within the area of Wyburton's personality, they were close friends, though (or perhaps because) when they talked, it was never of themselves, or of the operations of the present war; always of ideas — history; philosophy; with Marie sometimes, the Napoleonic idea; and often a subject they both cared about from different points of view — the rule of law. And they spent hours at piquet.

" Meanwhile Wyburton didn't take easily to Chassaigne who, he said, was a German-hater ' without the necessary coolness of steady distrust. . . . I don't like men who are emotional about danger,' he said. ' Their fears make them rash.' He was very far from recognizing Chassaigne as a member of the River Line, and the old fellow's curiosity about the outside world offended against his canons of security. I said: ' But France is Chassaigne's country. Do you blame him for wanting news of the places you have come through?' ' No,' said Wyburton, ' but he'll have to want. It would have been better,' he added, ' if Marie had let him believe that I was shot down as you and Frewer were.' But though he blamed Marie for having disclosed what kind of job he did, he said not a word of reproach to her; he thought it useless, I suppose, to go back over lost ground; anyhow, she wasn't his pupil and he had an inhuman capacity for not wasting his breath. Moreover, he recognized Marie as a fellow-professional with a command not subordinate to him. Knowing her repute in the network and the length of her service, he had great respect for her; to which personal liking was added.

" But, even with her, he could, on his own ground, be rigid and stubborn: absurdly so, I thought sometimes. He had a dagger-stick and nothing would separate him from it. Even when moving from one part of the granary to another, he carried it with him; he laid it across his legs when he sat in a chair to read or on the floor to play cards; he slept with it. 'Why?' Marie asked. 'Because it's my rule,' he said. When she persisted and laughed at him, he shut his mouth hard. Frewer mildly asked whether he might not become identifiable 'outside' as a man who always carried a stick. Wyburton rounded on him. 'Believe me, I don't repeat myself from trip to trip. There are other ways of carrying a long knife. You leave me to my trade.' After that we did."

It had been necessary, Sturgess had felt, to give Valerie his own view of Wyburton, even though she might think it wrong-headed. What he most ardently wanted her to understand was the strength, the solidarity and the essential happiness of the group at Blaise, and nothing was better evidence of this solidarity and its nature than the fact that Wyburton of all men had become part of it. The days which had followed Wyburton's arrival had been even happier than those which had preceded it.

"They were," Sturgess said, "brilliantly and quietly happy. I woke eagerly each morning, and slept every night with a sense, not of weariness or waste or discouragement, but of having grown and been refreshed by the living of that day. It sounds odd now; we read, we talked, played cards, went through our drill, did exercises — it sounds a futile, wasteful existence; and I used to ask myself then how it was that we five, American, English, French, thrown together by chance into what was, by any ordinary reckoning, a prison, found in it, not just a temporary refuge which we were glad of because we could lie and rest, but . . . a positive and fruitful virtue."

"It doesn't sound odd to me," Valerie said.

But Sturgess had need to convince himself. Not to be

active and yet to be positive and fruitful seemed, to what he called the crusading part of him, almost a contradiction in terms. " If I had been alone in feeling it," he replied, " I should have written it off as a personal freak. I'm a civilian at heart, I haven't the habit of war; it was open to anyone to say quite simply that I was glad to be out of it. But that explanation didn't hold water if you applied it to Wyburton who had the habit of war even to a fault, or to Heron, or to little Frewer who had all his courage rolled up tight into one symbol and had made his peace with fate. The charge of ' escapism ' applied to Marie least of all. You may say she was in love with Heron; probably she was; but that, in all the circumstances, might have been a torment. . . . No. . . . The value of our life there wasn't ' escape '; it wasn't negative at all.

" It was, I think," Sturgess went on, " the value of what Heron once called ' a creative pause '. In fact, he used the phrase in a different context. He wasn't talking about Blaise but about the probable exhaustion of the world after the war. The problem then, he said, wouldn't simply be that of choosing between one programme and another, or one economic system and another, or even between one form of government and another; it would be the problem of how to preserve in men the power to choose sanely. They were maddened by violent expedients and by the discovery that their ship no longer answered to the helm. The steering-gear itself — the power to choose and to think — had to be renewed. For that, the world was in desperate need of a period of creative pause.

" We debated the meaning and the possibility of that, ranging up and down history for parallel instances. Never until now, Heron argued, had there been the same necessity, because never before had man's knowledge so outrun his wisdom — his capacity to relate one knowledge to another knowledge, his capacity to synthesize. And never before had the whole world been maddened as it was now by a sense of frustration, of being separated from nature and from the very sources of self-renewal. The danger was much greater than what was ordinarily called a breakdown of civilization; civilizations had vanished before. The danger was of the disintegration of the human personality, the going-mad and the withering of man, because he was distracted and cut off from his roots. 'I mean by a creative pause,' Heron said, 'a period in which he regains his lost sense of origin, of rhythm and continuity, and in which he begins again to feel the sap rise. The idea of sap and the idea of fruit are not separable without madness, as spirit and nature are not, and the world in which we now exist is obsessed by the idea of fruit — and not even by the idea of bearing it but by the idea of consuming it. That is the insanity into which the economic interpretation of history has led us. Existence is economic, but life is not; that radical and vital contact has to be renewed.'

"At Blaise," Sturgess said, "it was renewed for us. I can't put it more clearly than by saying that we were happy in that way. Wyburton himself felt it, though he stated it concretely and, as you might expect, in terms of his own work. 'The remarkable thing about this place,' he said, 'is that our immediate, active purpose — to get out and get on — is so clearly defined, so completely prepared for, that it is, so to speak, finalized; we can forget about it. I find — I mean as regards my own job — that for once I can think back to the roots of policy instead of bothering my head about to-morrow's ways and means.' Marie heard him say that. She was always amused by his determination to think of everything in terms of his own job. 'You say "the roots of policy",' she said, 'meaning the policy of your own Service. But, you know, it goes further than that. Supposing I were to translate it *la sève de la vie*, what would you say to that?' '"The sap of life"?' Wyburton exclaimed. 'If you like. I don't quarrel with your translation.'

"That was the position," Sturgess said. "Call it a creative pause or what you will. Like your own relationship with your brother, it wasn't in the least intense, but we were bound together by it more closely than is at all common. It lasted, after Wyburton's coming, for just short of a fortnight. Then, as we had known it would, the end came abruptly."

24

"How did the end come?" Valerie asked, when Sturgess had been long silent.

Even then he did not reply at once, but gathered strength for what he had to say.

"One day about noon," he continued, "Marie told us we were to move that night. At the roadside trench where she had first found us, we were to be picked up and driven straight through to the frontier. Our preparations were made. We had nothing to do but wait.

"After supper, following our rule against carrying with us anything in writing, Heron and I carefully burned, one by one, scraps that we had written. We did it together, making sure that the charred fragments didn't blow about the granary; even they would show that the place had been recently inhabited, if ever it were searched. We collected the fragments in a china dish and were about to put them into the empty stove when the cautious Wyburton checked us. A stove, he said, was always searched; the charred paper must be taken out of the granary; so we left it for the moment in the china dish; later on, one of us would take it down to Chassaigne's room, together with a volume of Musset that I had borrowed from his shelves and must return.

"At that moment — it must have been half after nine — Marie came in. She had news from farther up the Line that the road which passed our trench had become unsafe; the enemy would move over it that night, and our transport had been diverted through Virac-St.-Just. We were to be at Meeting Place 46 — a grocer's shop in Virac — not earlier than one-five and not later than one-fifteen in the morning. Virac was forty-three kilometres east of Blaise, impossible on foot in the time. Secondary transport from Blaise to Virac had to be found. Marie couldn't drive; anyhow there wasn't a hope of stealing an automobile; even if she did and we drove it, she would be stranded at Virac, and the cat would be out of the bag. There were two possibilities: a truck that might be driven by Dessaix, a foreman at the Blaise brickworks; and a small Citroën belonging to the municipality that a certain Monsieur Félix, an official who had the key and a good name as a collaborator, might be persuaded to take out and drive for two perilous hours.

"They were loyal men, but the risks to them were enormous, and the greater because the notice was so short and they had no chance to prepare cover. 'It depends on how they are placed to-night,' Marie said. 'It may be impossible for either of them.' 'What would happen,' Wyburton asked, 'if we decided not to start?' Marie put that aside. 'If you stay here, either the whole Line will pile up now or within twenty-four hours I shall have eight men on my hands and the block at this end will be disastrous.' Wyburton, admitting that he didn't know the detail of the network and was speaking without his book, suggested that the Line would be more gravely endangered by sudden improvisation. Marie listened with a white, set face; then overruled him. The risks of our staying were, in her judgment, greater than the risks of our going. If she could persuade Dessaix or Félix to take us, we were to start. She would try Dessaix first; Félix's Citroën was dangerously small and Félix had a wife.

" She warned us that the arrangements she must now try to make would take time. She must approach the houses she had to visit with great caution. If Dessaix had company, she must make a plausible excuse for having called, leave him, watch the house, and return when his visitor had gone. So it might be with Félix if her first attempt failed. Time was short. Allow eight minutes for us to walk to the place to which the truck would come if it came at all. Allow a minimum of forty-five minutes for the journey. Total, fifty-three. We must leave not an instant after twelve-twenty-two. 'That,' Marie said, 'leaves no margin — none. It assumes an average speed of nearly sixty kilometres which is almost unworkable. I need fifteen minutes more. Take twelve-twenty-two as an extreme deadline. That gives me a little more than two hours and a half — more than enough if things go well; if not—' She held out her watch to Wyburton. 'Synchronize. . . . You are to be ready to start at sixty seconds' notice. Is it understood? . . . I may, if I have luck, be back in less than an hour. If I am not back by midnight—' Then with a sudden smile, at once bitter and childlike: 'I am sorry. It is not intelligent to operate without a margin. But we live in a world in which we have all agreed to be fooled by the clock.'

" When she was gone—"

The narrative halted abruptly, and silence again continued so long that Valerie at last repeated the last words he had spoken.

" I shall have to go back," he said. " There's too much you don't know. I suppose I was blind, wilfully blind. God knows, as I see it now, there was evidence enough, but I didn't see it so then."

He gave her the evidence, without comment, rehearsing the facts one by one as though he were reading them from a note-book: first, the governing fact that Heron, as an escaped prisoner of war, had appeared in Belgium without credentials; next, the incidents of the journey — his taking of old stamps and envelopes from the long-legged desk, his willingness to chatter with a German guard when they were travelling by bus, his buying of new stamps at the tobacconist's, his whispered conversation with the corporal; "and more than any of that, if I had had eyes to see," Sturgess said, "his queer boastfulness about his knowledge of German and Germany. Boastfulness of any kind was a contradiction in him; here it was designed, as a double bluff, to give cover to his Germanism. It succeeded with me. I think such suspicions as I had or might have had were always lulled by his parade of his German knowledge. If there had been anything wrong, it seemed to me that he wouldn't have dared to elaborate niceties of German scholarship with Chassaigne. He would have concealed rather than——"

She interrupted him. "Philip, you are talking beyond me. . . . Wrong? . . . Anything wrong? . . . What are you saying? What are you trying to prove?"

So deeply was his own thought entwined in the past that he looked towards her in astonishment. It was too dark now to see more than the shape of her face and the pale triangle of light between her body and a supporting arm.

"You will see," he said. "When Marie was gone, we were — for the first time, I think, since we came into the granary — at a loss. We wandered about aimlessly, all in the main part of the room. I was near the granary doors, thinking how delightful the place must have been when it was normally inhabited and the huge doors stood open on such a night as this. Heron was beside me. It was on my mind to say something, if I decently could, to indicate that Marie thought more about him than he took credit for. I wanted, I suppose, that he should at least say good-bye to her in some special way. How I should have said it I don't know. Quite suddenly he swung round and moved off towards the enclosed bit of the room, the Sardine Box. He lifted the curtain aside and went in. After a few minutes I remembered that the china dish containing our charred papers was still in the Box and decided to fetch it and take it to Chassaigne's room. When I reached the curtain and had put up my hand to draw it back, I was checked by what I saw.

" The two mattresses on which we used to sit sometimes had been rolled up and piled against the wall. The single armchair was still there but with its dust-sheet thrown over it to give it an appearance of disuse. The rug was on the floor; that was its permanent place; it wasn't ever moved except when we rolled it back to play cards. On the floor was the dark lantern we had used to burn our papers and beside it the china dish. Heron was squatting beside the lamp, with what seemed to be three or four sheets of half-folded paper in his hands. We had carefully turned out our pockets when we began our burning; carelessness in Heron wasn't to be expected; but there it was — these papers had been overlooked, I supposed; he had moved away from me into the Box, ashamed of having been careless, and was burning them now. So I thought. But it wasn't so. He wasn't unfolding them to burn. He was pressing them together — folding them, I mean, as you fold a letter before putting it into an envelope.

" He slid them into the left pocket of his jacket and almost at the same moment clapped his hand on to the right pocket, as though he had missed something. Then, moving his head slowly from side to side, looking for something lost, he began to straighten himself from his crouching position, to come up from the floor, and I knew that, already uneasy, he would in an instant become aware of being watched and look behind him. I turned away and walked straight out across the room. It was as intuitive as shutting your eyes against a blow in the face. I hadn't begun to reason. All I wanted was to avoid encounter with something that had become monstrous and contorted.

"Out there by the granary doors I came to a stand. The simplicity of it was that Heron intended, against the rule, to take papers out. . . . And if he did intend that? If he had deceived me, what then? Did it matter so much? Suppose that this were some writing of his, another poem perhaps, which he couldn't endure to destroy — wasn't that at any rate human and, except by the standard of our strict rule, a pardonable vanity? I tried to see it so. The remedy, then, was to tell him openly what I had seen and ask him to burn the papers he was carrying. I tried to quiet myself with that, but could not. The sense I had had of the monstrous and the perverse was shivering in me. I knew that the thing wasn't a poem or any innocent writing.

"Though I didn't then, I think, count up my earlier suspicions, their effect gave to what I had just seen a meaning of instant and sickening peril. The sense of evil was so extreme that it produced a reaction. I began to tell myself again that the thing would explain itself. In any case, I would free myself of the pressure of it. Wyburton and Frewer were within a few yards of me. When Heron came out of the Box, I would say in his hearing what I knew. It seemed for a moment gloriously simple. Anyhow it lifted the responsibility from me.

"A moment later Heron reappeared. He went over

to Frewer and began to talk to him. He glanced about him as though he was looking for something and slipped his hand into his inside breast-pocket, obviously in the thought that he might find there what he was seeking. I moved a step forward intending to speak; then halted and was silent.

" If I spoke out, Heron could pass the thing off — not without difficulty and embarrassment, it was true — but he could pass it off as a piece of vanity at most, apologize and burn the paper in his pocket. Wyburton would not insist on reading it; he had none of my earlier causes of suspicion. Even if I were to try to speak to Wyburton privately, which was possible but not easy in the circumstances of the granary, he would not and could not see the depths of the thing as I saw them. The notion that Heron was German and was acting for the Germans was completely alien to his thought. What evidence was there? Except in my recollection of the past, there was no evidence of anything more than a breach of our rule against carrying papers. Wyburton would think I had gone mad. Even the most elaborate argument would fail to rouse in him my long, cumulative fear, and elaborate argument wasn't possible. Even if he were convinced, or partly convinced, what then? What I wanted to do, naturally enough, was to *talk* — to Wyburton, to Heron, to all of them — but to talk; it was the last thing on earth that Wyburton himself would do if he were in my place. He would have enough sense — 'professional' sense if you like — not to blather at this stage. He would keep quiet and keep his eyes open. If I wasn't to lose my head and make a fool of myself, I must do the same.

" Whether it is ever wise to try to act by another man's pattern, I don't know, but I was out of my depth. I did what I thought Wyburton himself would have done. I kept quiet, let time pass, and then, as casually and unobtrusively as I could, crossed the room and went into the Box. The big room was pretty dark by then — only the remains of day striking down through the skylights, and the Box, shut in by bookcase and curtain, was darker, except where the lantern threw an arc across the floor. I went to the place where Heron had been. What I intended or hoped for in going there I scarcely know; one goes back to the unexplained, not so much in quest of explanation as fascinated by the gap that has opened in one's understanding. Heron, whom I had loved and honoured, had suddenly become — had become a gap in my estimate of human nature, and I returned, wanting not to have seen what I had seen, wanting my delusion to be still delusion, to the place where the gap had yawned. It was like going back on the day after a funeral to stare at the fresh grave.

"I crouched down as he had done, staring at the cracks in the floor-boards and the little fluff arising from them like illuminated, feathery trees, waving in the ground-draught; and behind the lamp, on its black side, in the blinded area between lamp and wall, there was a rectangle of paler darkness which, when I picked it up, I recognized as one of the blue envelopes that had been taken long ago from the long-legged desk. On it was written: Frau Gustav Keller, Lotzestrasse 73, Leipzig. It was stamped. It was empty, waiting for the letter which Heron had written. I read the address again and put the envelope back.

"To put it back had been my first impulse. I obeyed it. I think now I was right. Not to behave in any way that would warn Heron, to leave everything as it was until I had had time to think and act deliberately, was the idea to which I clung. Rightly or wrongly I put the envelope back and stood up. Even then I might have altered my decision. I was given no chance. Heron came in, the lamplight at waist-level. He had cards in his right hand. I said lamely: 'Are we going to play?' He answered: 'Wyburton suggested that we should. Better than watching the clock and waiting for the kettle to boil.' The naturalness of that saying seemed unnatural. He divided the cards and did a trick of his — shuffling them in the air by letting their corners flick against his two thumbs. 'I suppose this will be our last game,' he said. The horrible thing is that the word 'last' took me by the throat. I wanted to go up to him and take his arm and say: Look, Heron, this is hell, this is madness, and be reconciled with him, but I knew I couldn't. I was choking with frustrate sentiment and with the fear of that sentiment — the fear of taking a false step, of blurting out everything for the sake of ridding myself of the burden of it. I distrusted myself; my eyes were stinging, a rivulet of sweat was running down the inside of my right upper arm; I couldn't be still. So I passed him and went out.

"Wyburton was moving in, Frewer behind him. Wyburton was leaning heavily on his stick; he had made himself appear high-shouldered and clumsy, and had pinched on to his nose the pair of rimless glasses which, he had said once, were more valuable as disguise than a thousand false beards. He said they changed the character of his face; it was true. Together with pursed mouth and teeth clipped down on the lower lip, they gave him what he called 'the appearance of a bureaucratic rabbit'. Now, at sight of me, he played his part, speaking French in that tone of highly reasonable grievance with which small French officials vindicate the Rights of Man. The manner was faultless; the matter, the wildest nonsense — brilliant Alice-in-Wonderland fooling. Frewer was helpless with quiet, bubbling laughter. To me, the episode, coming then, was a blazing grotesque. I tried to speak. Wyburton wouldn't listen. No seriousness will hold back laughter on its crest. I seized his arm, thinking to recall and steady him. Hopeless. He believed, like a kitten, that I was entering into his game and played back. Utterly hopeless. At that moment, he was incapable of understanding that I had something of importance to say. Suddenly he bowed — the sharp, ironic bow of a bureaucratic rabbit — lifted a polite invisible hat, slid past me, and went into the Box. There was nothing to do but follow him.

" Heron had rolled back the rug and moved the lamp out on to the area of floor that was to be our card-table. The envelope of course was gone. Frewer brought out a bowl of chips by putting his arm round the end of the bookcase to the shelf in front where the bowl was always hidden. The game was poker. We sat down and began to deal. ' Not quite eleven,' Wyburton said. ' It looks as if she hadn't clicked with Dessaix.' Little Frewer arranged his hand. ' Come on,' he said. ' Let's play. Your ante, Sturgess. . . .' Then he added in the rather languid, toneless way that had irritated me once: ' That girl has guts. It must be hell to do her job alone.'

" I was calm now. Perhaps what Frewer said calmed me. If what I believed to be true was true, if Heron was what my Belgian had spoken of as *un faux Anglais* who had introduced himself into the Line in order to observe its working from Brussels to the Pyrenees, if his intention was to see the whole thing from end to end and either to vanish at the Spanish frontier or even to cross it, we — Frewer, Wyburton and I — should be allowed to go through, or might be. Marie would be trapped. Not she only, but everyone who had helped us in the Line. It was she who must be told.

"My poker is good. It always has been. Sounds odd, but I believe it has never been steadier or better. It had, too, the effect of draining away panic, and I began to think clearly.

"It had been early in our travels that Heron had taken the envelopes and stamps from the long-legged desk. Therefore he had probably intended early communication with Germany. As France was an occupied country, full of Germans sending letters home, there was no difficulty of communication; and for him, travelling by a route of which he had no previous knowledge and without the possibility of pre-arranged contacts with his own agents, the open post was the best method of communicating. But why had he delayed so long? It was true that he needed envelopes and stamps; knowing that he might be searched by the River Line, he wouldn't have carried French stamps with him out of Germany. But, once he had them, why had he delayed? An ingenious notion, too ingenious perhaps, came into my mind: that the stamps he found had lain too long in the desk and, for one reason or another, were unusable; perhaps the gum was rotten and they wouldn't stick. Anyhow, he had bought others. Even so, why had he delayed until now?

"The thought gripped me that perhaps he hadn't. Interim reports might already have gone back and what he had in his pocket be the last of a series. If his plan was not to break away from us in France but to cross into Spain and observe our contacts there, it was to be expected that he should send back a report before crossing the frontier. But he might also have sent earlier reports. If so, the earlier stages of the River Line were already compromised, but not yet the later. Nothing about

Blaise had gone out. If Marie were warned and Heron kept prisoner, she at least would be safe and might even be able to send warnings up the Line before the enemy struck.

" It was then that a picture swam into my mind of a happening which, until that moment, I had completely misinterpreted — a picture of Heron, on the night when Wyburton was expected, trying to persuade Marie to let him go with her out of the granary, out into the open. Obviously, whatever his motive had been, it had not been to protect her. All my evidence converged. Everything that had happened for weeks past was given a new meaning by the letter to Lotzestrasse.

" As soon as I grasped this, I was a thousand times glad that I had kept my mouth shut. This wasn't Wyburton's affair. Far better that Heron should remain unsuspecting and that Marie should be told. Dessaix, Félix — how far they were to be depended on I didn't know, but presumably there was help she could call upon in Blaise or near it. She had command at any rate of her own network of communications. The responsibility was hers and my responsibility was to her. So I saw it then. So I see it now.

" Meanwhile I was playing poker like a book. Left in with Heron and holding good fours, I went away before what turned out to be a straight flush. ' Good God,' he said, ' what on earth told you not to bet ? ' I had to look at him then ; I hadn't since we sat down to play ; and it seemed to me incredible and shocking that he was unchanged — the same erectness of position, the same steadfastness of manner, the same good humour, the same undefinable power to win affection and confidence. Frau Gustav Keller, Lotzestrasse 73. Who was she ? I saw her knitting in a room full of plaster busts. The bust of Wagner with his floppy hat. Why I don't know. My idea of a German interior, I suppose. Just the plaster busts, and her hands knitting, and a central parting in her hair — not her face. Who was she? Not that it mattered; probably a post-box, no more; probably Heron had never seen her; she was an address — Lotzestrasse 73. It didn't matter who she was, but I saw the crown of her head, the knitting-needles, the figures Seven and Three in brass under a door-knocker, and Leipzig — a black blob on the map of Germany. . . . We were playing a jack-pot. It was my turn, and I said no. No one would open. We threw in the cards. Queen-pot. . . . What did Lotze mean? Was it a man's name? I had a vague idea that it was the name of a philosopher. If I said to Heron: Heron, you know German. What does Lotze mean? . . . 'Yes,' Wyburton said, 'I open a king-pot.' . . . I was thinking that way. Two thoughts, three, four thoughts at once. Always knowing I must act. Always dreaming myself into inaction.

"I did nothing. I didn't move except to take cards or deal them. I didn't move because the habit of one's mind dies so infernally hard. I'm not, I hope, in the blatant sense, a wishful thinker. I don't believe that things will happen because I want them to. But I am a wishful not-thinker. Who isn't? I exclude certain things — things that won't happen to me; things I shall never do. I shall not murder; I shall not be blackmailed; the things that happen to people in newspapers won't happen to me. The men and women I love won't turn into devils. I shan't ever sit in a machine at night and drop bombs on cities. Others may; I shan't. One thinks that way; then the thing happens; one does sit in a machine and drop bombs; but one goes on thinking that way. I knew well enough what Heron had done and what he was.

There wasn't room for doubt. No British officer, escaping down the River Line, could have an honest reason to post a letter to Lotzestrasse 73. I didn't have to count my earlier suspicions and add them; they flooded up — or, rather, Lotzestrasse 73 seeped down into them. But when I looked at Heron, though my intelligence was clear, my *self*, my being, wouldn't accept that this thing had irretrievably happened, was happening, to me, and that I, as if I were another person, as if I were Wyburton, had to act in conformity with it and act now and act alone.

" Wyburton looked at his watch. It was eleven-eighteen. He was dealer and offered me cards. I took three, a queen, a jack, a seven, and threw in all five. I said: 'Leave me out of the next hand. I'll take that china dish and the book down to Chassaigne.'

" He was in bed, as he had been on the first night. There was a book open on the coverlet, but it was not being read. He had forgotten about it and let it slide. There it was, still open, its white pages staring up at the ceiling from the wrong slope of his knees. As I went in, he looked at me as a fish looks at you out of an aquarium tank. He slowly remembered what I was — one of the savages in his roof; and smiled with his teeth and his moustache — not at me, I was anonymous still, but at the irrational fantasy that had rained savages on to this glassy old age.

" 'She is not back,' he said.

" I put down the Musset, emptied the dish into his basket, and dragged a chair close up to his bedside. 'I lie here,' he said. 'I lie here. She goes out. I am never sure that she will return. There is nothing I can do. I have written nothing all day. There is nothing I can do.' His hand was opening and closing on the coverlet, kneading it, like a cat's paw.

"I have never seen a man so lonely. He was like a scolded child shut up in his room, but it was all life that had scolded him. To gather his attention was my first care and I said: 'Listen. There is something very urgent that you can do.'

"Ah, but he was quick! The French have an unparalleled quickness and directness. No buts, no wandering, no woolliness . . . no pity for enemies. *On les aura.* . . . While I spoke, he did not interrupt. When I had done, he said: 'My friend, what you tell me does not surprise me of that man.' Then after so long a pause that I thought his mind had strayed, he said: 'Leipzig. . . . Well?'

"I wasn't quick enough. I didn't know that, in that one word, was all resolve. 'Well?' he said, meaning: it is settled, it is done, why are you loitering here? I was too slow for the leap of his mind, and began to explain laboriously what I expected of him. Marie, returning to us, must pass through his room. Would he tell her fully what I had told him so that she might be forewarned? Was it clear to him? I asked doubtfully. Would he be sure to tell her? 'You see,' I said, 'it may be necessary for her to inform others and consider what is best to be done. It is clear that Heron must be kept under guard, here or elsewhere.'

"Chassaigne hauled up the book from his knees, closed it, and caressed its leather binding with flat, taut hands. I remember it because he made no other movement, and the bending back of those long-nailed fingers and the soft grating of his palms was, in some unspeakable way, ecstatic. '*Il ne passera pas*,' he said, which I understood to mean that Heron should not go. It didn't occur to me then that he was thinking of Weitbrecht and of Verdun.

"This satisfied me. I had done what I had to do and

returned to the granary. It needed an effort to sit down again in the Box and take a hand; a greater effort to play it intelligently. It had been six minutes to midnight when I came up from Chassaigne's. We played on as steadily as we could, but time began to shout in our ears. There was a moment when even Wyburton shook. He put down the pack and drew one of those sharp, dragging sighs that people sigh in their sleep; an instant later he had a grip on himself. 'Twelve-seven,' he said, 'ye gods, she is running it fine.' We shifted, the game would have broken up, but he wouldn't allow it. He slid the pack to Frewer and said: 'Cut to Heron.'

" I resolved not to look again at my watch. Twelve-twenty-two was Marie's deadline. We played like machines, except Heron, who appeared to be untroubled. When Marie came into her father's room I'm not sure. I was listening but may have missed her coming. At last I did hear movement below. Then voices for a moment, then nothing. He's telling her now, I thought, and was in an agony because I knew how long it must take to tell her all there was to be told and for her to decide what to do.

" While I was thinking this, and after an interval of time so short that its shortness is a thing that even now I don't understand, I heard her climb the ladder and enter the granary. She pulled back our curtain and entered the Box. It was twelve-eighteen. We were all looking in her direction. The others had begun to stand up. I hadn't; I knew we couldn't leave instantly; there were things she must say or do, whatever her decision might be. To Julian Wyburton only one idea was possible: that she had come for us, that we were perilously late and must go. He gave the evacuation order: 'Sixty seconds.' She countermanded it: 'No,' and repeated: 'No.' Julian and Frewer told me afterwards that they saw no sign of emotion in her. I saw her move her tongue over her lips, twice. 'There is a hitch. Sit down. Go on with your game,' she said, and sat down with us.

"She chose her place, between Wyburton and me, facing Heron. I supposed that she would now ask him for an explanation.

"Instead she was silent, her eyes for a moment shut, screwed up tight. Her right hand closed on her left wrist as though she were gripping terror by the neck and strangling it. Her eyes opened very wide and she said: 'Commander!'

"She never addressed Julian by his rank, and the effect was as clear, definite and instantaneous as the movement of a starting-lever in a faultless machine. I can't describe it in terms of any physical change in him. His limbs didn't move or his eyes, but somehow that one word produced in him an absolute alertness that was to me at the same time wonderful and — shocking? 'Yes,' was all he answered.

"Then she said — she needn't have, I think; Julian was fully prepared — but she said: 'You have sworn obedience.'

"He didn't answer, but moved his shoulder muscles, stiffening himself for whatever was to come.

"Then she released her wrist, lifted her right arm towards Heron, lifted her body with it — it was a kind of shuddering elongation like the yielding of a racked limb, and said: 'Kill that man.'

"Julian drove one hard breath outward through his teeth, like the whistle of his dagger coming out, and sprang. Heron died without a sound except the last surge in his throat and one beat of his knuckles on the ground. As he went, I saw his eyes. Incredulous, Julian says. That's true. But more: not trapped, not weighed down, not darkened. . . . I can't say it. . . . Light — and light-bringing ? "

Sturgess paused on that interrogation, asking her for understanding, and asking himself. Then he brought his tale to an end with a curious lameness. He let it peter out.

" When Julian stood up from what he had done, and Frewer was staring and staring with his hands laid flat against his cheeks and his lips pushed forward, Marie said : ' Come. Follow.' And, looking at me : ' He will tell you. . . . Follow.'

" We went through none of our evacuation drill. We left the cards, the chips, the rug rolled back. Too much. Too much to be done. . . . The whole room stiff and mad, time gone. . . . Julian stretched his wrist-watch into the lamp-beam. I saw it. Twelve-twenty-four. We went down through Chassaigne's room — he said nothing but his eyes were counting us — through the passages, the gallery, across the stone flags, into the open. So on. So on. Félix's Citroën. Marie going back to her home. Félix would convoy us to Virac. She didn't say good-night. Nor we. Nothing was said. We drove away. At Virac we made the contact. There was difficulty. They had expected four. Why were there three, not four? We couldn't give the reason. We said ' a broken ankle ' and they accepted it. There was a big Renault waiting. . . . All that night we couldn't speak of what had been done. Our new driver couldn't be allowed to know. We drove for hours in silence. Once Julian said : ' Marie will have to do alone what has to be done. Clear up the mess.' "

25

EAGER that the morning sun should wake him, Sturgess slept that night with the curtains drawn back from his bedroom windows. He was up early, and went out into the air, restless with happiness. The telling of his story to the end had been the casting-off of a load heavier than he had known until he was free of it.

Valerie had received his tale with the utmost simplicity, neither praising his decisiveness nor condemning the violence that had been its result. The first words she spoke, gentle towards him but unstressed, had released the tension of his mind. She had disregarded his obsession, walked through his ghosts, and, at the same time, not held aloof from him. She could have done him no service more loving.

Her action had been as candid and steady as her speech. When they were standing on the wood-path and he offered to return with her, she had put her arm in his, and said no, to-night she would go on with him until he was " out of the wood ", then find her own way back; and he had accepted her friendly firmness. " You have been thinking of it all too—" she had broken off smilingly to coin a word—" too *complicatedly*: haven't you? Like people who lie awake because they have figures running in their head? " He had admitted it, and gradually, as they walked on together, the episode had freed itself from the entanglements of personal right and personal pride;

he had begun to see it, as she did, in the perspective of a tragedy greater than its own; and her serenity, comparable with Heron's, gave him understanding, as nothing else could have done, of the quality of her feeling for him. Love gave to her youth a wisdom different from that of age, which is the wisdom of an old tree; it gave to her the deep, animating charity of root and sap; and he felt it flow from her to him.

Before they reached the edge of the wood she had even led him into talking of other things, then had halted. Could he find his own way home? . . . Indeed, he could. . . . And sleep with a quiet mind? . . .

Now, in the morning sunlight, as he was looking out towards the edge of the wood where she had parted from him, he saw Julian come out from it and begin to climb the intervening field.

"You're early," Julian said as he came up.

"You are earlier."

"But I'm a working man. What is more, I went early to bed. . . . Was yours a pleasant evening?"

Sturgess nodded. "It ended well."

"That's as it should be. . . . Let's go in to breakfast. Is Marie down?"

"Not yet, I think. I haven't seen her."

While they drank their coffee, Tucker came in with the morning's letters. His distribution of them was a daily ritual, conducted with benign deliberateness as though each letter were a gift that he had detached from a Christmas tree. So slow was the process that Julian was each morning silently infuriated by it, and when at last it was over and Tucker gone, he turned his pile of letters on to their faces with an impatient slap, ripped them open with a paper-knife, pulled out their contents, heaped them, and began to read.

" You're too efficient," Sturgess said. " You don't know how to enjoy your mail."

Julian glanced up but continued to read. Not until he had scanned each letter did he push them all aside and reach for the coffee-pot.

" Sorry. . . . Now I can be human. . . . I have to go into Bath to-day. Do you want to come with me? There's no earthly reason that you should."

" I'm going up-river."

" Same charming company ? "

" Yes."

" Good. . . . Have you told her the whole tale, Philip ? "

" Yes."

" All of it ? "

" Yes. Do you mind ? "

" N—no. Not if you're going to marry her. Are you ? "

" I shall find out to-day."

To this Julian gave no response but a tautening of the muscles at the sides of his mouth.

" There's one thing I want to ask. When you have told the Blaise story — elsewhere, I mean; in America for example — have you given my name ? "

" Your Christian name; never more."

" Good. And Heron's ? "

" In fact, no. I have always called him Heron. I think of him so."

" To her also ? "

" Yes," said Sturgess. " The name, Lang, was false. It never enters my mind. Anyhow what odds would it make ? "

Julian hesitated; then said: " Is there anything to be gained by letting the enemy know what became of their agents ? "

This obsession of secrecy after the event was familiar enough, and Sturgess let it go without comment. Marie came into the room, and of Heron no more was said.

There were hours to pass after breakfast before Sturgess could reasonably present himself at Mrs. Muriven's house. He spent them in writing to his mother the opening pages of a letter which, he believed, would be the most important that he had ever written. It was intended to be an extremely solemn and filial letter. He wanted his mother to understand that Valerie, though she had inevitably an English accent, was innocent of that high-pitched, drooping voice which made some Englishwomen sound as if they were half choked by a diamond dog-collar and talking over the edge of it to a puppy on the mat. Her voice on the contrary — and he told how, before he had seen her, he had been struck by the warmth and generosity of her voice. "Do you understand what I mean by the generosity of a voice? I think you do. You have it yourself. Southern in tone — though of course without the queer lift which makes all sentences in South Carolina end in a question-mark??" His mother would laugh at that, being herself half-Carolinian and knowing well that that very question-mark, in the voice of the deep South, had been before now dangerous music in his ears; and his letter, which he had intended to be solemn, fortunately strayed from a catalogue of Valerie's virtues into a confident lightness of heart. The last words he wrote were: "I am going to meet her now. More when I return."

He looked at his watch, gazed at the blank area of paper on which this evening his happy fortune would be recorded, and strode out to meet that fortune. "Thursday" was written at the top of his letter, and that encouraged him. He had been born on a Thursday, and, being an optimist, still regarded it as his lucky day.

Mrs. Muriven, gloved and booted, was gardening in front of her house.

" Valerie," she said, " is at this moment carrying your basket down to the boat. Come through the house. I have a glass of sherry to put you on your way."

They went into the living-room, and Mrs. Muriven leaned out of the window to call in Valerie from the lawn. Then, turning back, she said:

" She goes on Sunday."

" Lord Almighty, is that so ? "

" Her passage was confirmed by telephone this morning. She leaves here on Sunday. That will give her one clear day in London. She goes on board on Tuesday afternoon."

" Well," Sturgess said, " thank you for the warning."

" Does it disturb you ? I don't think it should."

" Passages can be cancelled."

Mrs. Muriven looked at him as she might have looked at a too impetuous boy. " Unwise," she said.

" Unwise ? "

" To press for that. Believe me. She will wish to go through with what she has undertaken — at any rate for a little while until her brother has a chance to make alternative arrangements at his end."

The assumption underlying this advice amused and delighted Sturgess.

" Aren't you taking something for granted ? "

" It was you who suggested the cancellation of passages."

" True. . . . In America, you know, we like to move fast."

" Indeed you do. That is why I spoke. Here is your sherry." The door from the garden opened and shut.

" And here is your Englishwoman." A little emphasis on the last word.

She was a wise old lady, no doubt, and knew her world; but South Africa was a long way off, and he was impatient, seeing indefinite months stretch ahead. Nevertheless, hearing Valerie's step and remembering last night, he faithfully resolved not to allow his impatience to urge her against her judgment. He would be content to wait if she wished it; he would even be peacefully content. At least, he thought so then, having before him a long, happy day in her company.

" Well," he said quietly, " here's to the return passage," and turned, glass in hand, as the door began to open.

26

THE river was narrow and not deep. Twice, above Tarryford bridge, they ran aground and pushed off into the channel again.

" If this were the Hudson," Sturgess exclaimed, as he took soundings with an oar, " I should do better. And if I didn't, I should be less ashamed."

" The Tarry," she answered, " isn't designed for speed."

" Still I don't like to be made a fool of by a small river. Look at it! Smooth and innocent on the surface, but every yard of it a trap for mariners. Where is this Radlett's Island ? "

She pointed vaguely ahead.

" I don't see there's room for an island."

" Oh, but it doesn't sit in midstream. It is formed —" she lay back and laughed — " by two branches of a tributary."

" Impossible," he said, " the Tarry can't have tributaries outside Lilliput."

But the tributary appeared, and the Tarry, with a graceful bend and a glint of stony shallows, widened to receive it. It was a wood-stream, appearing through a tunnel of branches to form a gently agitated pool of light and leaf-green and there to divide into two rivulets, each running down a side of a triangular island of which the base was the Tarry itself. Here they tied up the boat, carried their basket to the edge of the island-copse where they might have shade or sunshine at will, and began to idle away what remained of the forenoon.

To watch the river and to hear it in their silences, to exchange remembrances, ideas, tastes, hopes — in brief, to learn each other, was their happiness then — a happiness so expectant and so carefree that Sturgess was in no haste to ask her the direct question to which in his mind, and he did not doubt in her mind also, the day was leading. His asking and her giving a pledge would but lend words to what was already felt to exist between them, and the words, he thought, when they came, would arise spontaneously, without being designed or summoned, from the drifting chances of conversation and stillness. Better so; for then they might have, or seem to have, what choice could not give them: the natural poetry there was in being that day alive and together, with all the months of their years and all the minutes of that afternoon lying ahead.

So he allowed their talk to wander where it would, untroubled even when, as they drank coffee after luncheon, she returned for a moment to the subject of Blaise.

" Do you think," she asked, " that he did in fact send home an earlier letter and that Marie's arrest may indirectly have been the result? "

" Not Marie's arrest. That was independent of him," Sturgess replied, turning on his face and balancing his coffee-cup among the grasses. " She says so, and I have no doubt of it. But that he did send back an earlier letter we know. The astonishing thing is that Dick Frewer knew of it; so he told us when we were on our way home. He knew and he let it pass. Heron, he said, told him voluntarily and gave what seemed at the time a convincing explanation. The ' voluntarily ' is of course absurd in the light of what happened afterwards. Presumably Heron thought that Dick had suspicions and, knowing that the boy was under his spell, took this bold way of quieting them. And the explanation was pretty ingenious."

He sat up again and returned his empty cup to the basket; then, while he filled his pipe, continued: "One of his fellow-prisoners in Germany, Heron said, had been a young British major of Jewish blood with a conspicuously Jewish name. He had a sister — the only near relation he possessed — living in Germany and married to a German. She had concealed her Jewish origin and, for her sake, he didn't dare communicate with her through the prison-camp censorship. But he was dying; there were things he had to tell her — personal things and business things; and when he knew that Heron was about to escape, he asked Heron to act for him. What was to be said had to be carried in Heron's memory; but once in France he could write it down — the business details first, so he told Frewer, leaving the personal messages for a later stage."

"He told Frewer. Why didn't Frewer tell you?"

Sturgess shrugged his shoulders. "I understand that. He regarded it as a personal confidence of one Englishman to another."

"Even so," Valerie said, "surely, if Heron had been genuine, his right course would have been to explain the circumstances to Marie, or to whatever member of the River Line was in charge of you, and ask for the letter to be read and sent?"

"I thought that. On balance, I still think so," Sturgess replied. "But Frewer took the other view, and I admit it wasn't unreasonable. Most of the River Line agents, unlike Marie, were people we never got to know; anyhow they were automata, obeying strict rules, exercising no discretion of their own. To give a letter to them was to take a ten to one chance against its ever being sent; so he told Frewer instead. . . . That, anyhow, is the way Frewer saw it. I dare say he was flattered; anyhow, he was persuaded; and assuming, as he did, that Heron was as English as he was himself, it wasn't against reason."

"And the second letter?" Valerie asked. "The one Heron would have sent from Blaise?"

"I don't yet know the details of it," Sturgess answered. "I haven't discussed it with Marie. All I know I know indirectly, through Julian. She says that the letter appeared to be harmless and was written to a woman about her brother. She says, too, that when she had it tested for cipher by the River Line cryptographers the early results were negative. Beyond that she hasn't gone; maybe, she can't; she herself was arrested soon afterwards. . . . In any case, that letter was found by her on Heron's body. Everything associated with it in her mind must be part of a nightmare. Unless she talks of it of her own free will, there's little I can decently ask."

Soon after this, talking of happier things, they climbed down into the boat, moved a little way upstream, landed, and explored the wood above the tributary, coming out upon high, open ground and a fresh blaze of sunlight. The early afternoon was gone when they returned to the island.

"You see," she said unexpectedly, "your story, if one thinks about it, raises questions which simply didn't exist in our grandparents' time. They had their own problems, heaven knows, but to them what they called 'melodrama' was a kind of absurdity — anyhow completely fictitious or wildly exceptional, outside normal experience. And we live in it. We still try to pretend that we don't, but in fact we do. The things that used to appear only in fantastic stories have become commonplaces:

war, assassination, torture, bombs raining from the sky, espionage, cryptography, the ruthless, systematic betrayal of personal loyalties — all commonplaces; with the result that a girl living in her own home, where she was brought up as a child, finds herself doing what Marie had to do, and you and Julian Wyburton and Heron himself — all of you found yourselves doing things, right and inevitable things on that plane of insane violence, which were opposed to every intuition of your personal lives. It *is* madness, Philip."

"But the world," he said, "has gone through its periods of violence before."

"Different from this."

"In what way different?"

"The violence was slower and far less penetrating. There weren't the same communications to carry it — and, what is worse, the perpetual thought of it. There were huge areas of life in which men thought in terms of their flocks and herds, their families, their village, and into those areas violence came only as a special misfortune. Now violence isn't a special misfortune: it is a condition of thought. The arbitrary and the brutal and the unknowable are forcing their way into *all* life like some black river flooding into men's homes and choking them. That is new."

"If so," he answered, "it may produce new remedies."

"For example?"

He said questioningly: "Some kind of world federation? An agreement, little by little, to surrender national sovereignties? Do you rule that out?"

"No," she answered, "but I don't believe it will come now, as it might possibly have come after the last war, by what my brother used to call 'soft policy'. He said the issues had hardened. He thought that 'open diplomacy' had changed negotiation into howling propaganda and made agreement on those lines impossible. Even disarmament had ceased to be a means of conciliation and had become an invitation to banditry. I believe he was right. The world is caught as you were caught; you couldn't wait and argue and discuss; on that plane of violence you had to take responsibility as Heron had to take risk."

" I remember," Sturgess interposed, " a discussion with him that troubled me then and troubles me even more now — now, I mean, that the whole future of mankind depends upon whether the United States uses, or abstains from using, the atomic bomb as an instrument of policy. Heron was arguing that what he called the Obsessed Men — the Nazis and the Communists — believed that the liberal world of the West had lost the will to maintain its own defence. ' But it is defending itself,' I said. He smiled at that. ' I know,' he answered, ' but only at the last, desperate moment. The theory of the Obsessed Men is that the West, even if it should win this time, will not use its strength to safeguard itself; it will sit back and disarm, and play for comfort and self-righteousness, and then once more, allowing its enemies to choose their own time, fight at every possible disadvantage to defend its weakness. The calculation is that in the end the West must lose that gamble because it hasn't the moral courage to use power when it has power to use.' Then Heron used a phrase which sticks in my mind: ' Power that is not mad must be used in restraint of power that is.' And Marie, looking at me, said with a smile: ' You, as a good American, ought to remember your Montesquieu: " *Il faut que le pouvoir arrête le pouvoir.*" Your constitution was built on that.'

" I argued with Heron — pretty desperately. I am a natural conciliator. I loathe the very idea of using power internationally while there's one per cent hope that it may not have to be used. And anyway, I asked, who was to decide whether power was mad or sane? Was each man and each nation to be judge in its own cause? And Heron answered: yes, to be judge in one's own cause was to exercise conscience; but a judge didn't make the law, he interpreted it; and in the same way, the exercise of conscience was evil and fanatical and insane if it *made* law; its task was to interpret a known law, to apply principles in essence religious to particular cases, not to decide each case on a basis of self-will."

" Did Heron say that?" Valerie replied quietly. " My brother so often said it in different words. . . ." She picked up her bag from the grass at her side and pressed it between her hands and wrists. Then, looking at Sturgess with a long gaze at once penetrating and shy, as though she were indeed looking for her fate in him, she said: " One German; the other English; both dead; and you and I still living. It's almost as if we had been pupils of the same master."

Sturgess would have spoken then. The chance had come; but she took from her handbag a small folded leather case and slid it a few inches towards him.

" That was my brother," she said, and looked away down-river.

Curious chiefly for a resemblance to her, he undid the press-button which held the case shut and flicked it open in the palm of his left hand. The face that looked out at him was Heron's.

Heron was her brother, his mind said, but at first he was numb as one is numb at the first news of death. Heron was her brother, his mind repeated. Then, suddenly his mind cried out: Heron was innocent! It was as if he had been walking in sunlight and great needles, out of the air, had been thrust into the eyes of his mind.

If she had been watching him at the moment of impact, concealment of his knowledge would have been impossible, but he was given time. Out of the darkness and silence he was able to say:

"What was his name?"

"John. John Lang. I told you — he was my half-brother."

To gain more time, he asked meaningless, conventional questions: what uniform her brother was wearing, what his age had been — and while he asked and she answered, he saw in imagination, enclosed in the blotter on his bedroom writing-table at Stanning, the partly written letter to his mother which could never be finished.

"Philip, my dear, what is the matter?"

"Nothing."

"But there is something."

"No."

But he could not conceal his face from her.

"You look ill. Why? What has happened?"

She would have taken his hand, but he prevented her by closing the photograph-case and returning it. There was nothing he could ask that he would have asked and no explanation he could offer. He had receded from her across an unbridgeable gulf into his private silence and darkness. He would not drag her down after him into the blinded pit of his self-knowledge. He would at least be alone in this. Springing to his feet, he went down to the boat and began to draw it in; then straightened himself, painter in hand, and looked at the sickened enchantment of the sun, the river, the island, all emptied of their morning's delight, and heard behind him the morning-sound of the plashing "tributary", and heard again in memory — as he would all his life hear again and again — her laughter at the word.

"I think," he said as steadily as he could, "we had better go back. Will you forgive me?"

They went downstream almost in silence. When they ran aground as they had on their way up, they tried to laugh over the mishap and failed. As he rowed, their eyes continually encountered, and he saw in hers the same incredulous acceptance that had been in Heron's as he died.

"Something has happened," she said. "If you can, tell me."

But he gave only stiff, conventional denials and she asked no more. He understood with terror that it was her love for him, the strange paralysis of love when it is incomprehensibly wounded, that withheld her from pressing for the explanation which would have been a natural demand between friend and friend. Tears came into her eyes, but she made herself mistress of them, and with a lovely, easing discretion broke the tension of their silences with unagonized talk.

Divine good manners! The supreme grace of not driving life into a corner and making a scene there! In return, there was one thing he had to say — to be clear, to be honest as he saw it, to make an ending: "It is true that you leave on Sunday?"

"Yes."

"Then this — unless by chance — is good-bye."

For a long time, she did not speak and he dared not look at her. Then her voice — it was Heron's voice, as the carriage of her head and the long grace of her movement were his also — said gently:

" Good-bye, dear Philip. . . . I mean it in the old sense."

" The old sense ? "

" God be with you, my dear, in all your strange troubles, and with me in mine."

His hands loosened on the oars, but he hardened his resolution, which he felt to be binding upon him, and rowed on.

27

DURING the day, Julian, encountering Mrs. Muriven in the village, had been told that Valerie would leave Tarryford on Sunday. In the belief that he was doing his guest a good turn, he had invited both ladies to dine at Stanning on Saturday evening. When he told Sturgess this, the reply was: "Bless you, Julian, that was good of you, but I think they won't come."

"The old lady accepted. She said that Valerie's packing would be disposed of before then."

"Still, I think they won't come."

After one quick, shrewd look, Julian forbore to ask why and switched the conversation away. The Wyburton silence had closed like an iron gate. Unless I deliberately speak of her, Sturgess thought, Valerie's name will never be spoken in this house again.

Friday was the hardest of days. He checked a wild impulse to pack his bags and go. Instead he demanded work, manual work, and was given it in abundance, and in the evening the three of them discussed politics until after eleven. It was a good discussion, so enlivened by Marie's intelligence that he enjoyed it while it lasted, but, when he reached his bedroom, he was visited by that sense of life's withdrawal, of having been left high and dry, which makes an absurdity of all endeavour — of the struggle of statesmanship equally with the little effort required to undress and go to bed; and he sat at his writing-table in desperate inaction, quite still, his limbs cramped, while moths came in from the summer's night and fluttered about him.

The price that he must pay for the error he had made was to carry alone the secret of it. That Heron had been an English officer wrongly killed was a burden of truth that Julian and Marie must never be allowed to share; no gain, except the weak sterile pleasure of whining to someone, could result from his telling them, and their marriage might well be broken by the knowledge. Whether he told Valerie or not, his marriage with her had been made impossible; and to tell her would scar her thought of her brother with the ugliness and futility of his end.

Sturgess offered no querulous protest against the fate which bound him to silence and made impossible marriage with the woman whose brother he had killed; for he recognized it as being indeed the working out of destiny, not the hazard of misfortune or coincidence.

Tragedy, he had learned to say long ago without more than intellectual understanding of what he said, does not consist in misfortune or in unhappiness; these may be the accidents of tragedy, but they are not the tragic essence. Tragedy consists in the conflict within man of good with good, of his arrogance within that disharmony, of his proud emphasis on one duty to the neglect of another, of his attempt to cut his way out of his predicament by killing or sterilizing a part of himself; and his failure to resolve his inward conflict is visited alway by penalties which — which destroy him, the Greeks had seemed to say sometimes, or which, Sturgess's own hopeful spirit had added, man may suffer and pass through to his own salvation, his reconciliation with the gods. The Greeks themselves had often appeared to hold out this promise: in the *Eumenides* perhaps, in the *Oedipus Coloneus* certainly, and he clung to it as a link between the Greek and the Christian wisdom.

What he had done at Blaise had not been wrong within the limits of his knowledge, and there was, he knew, a rational argument that would pronounce him to be, therefore, guiltless; but it was an argument that he could no longer apply to himself. Absence of knowledge was not an acceptable plea of innocence. It had never been so among the Greeks or in nature. I did not know! I did not mean it! was a cry to which Fate was deaf. Tragedy might not always demand catastrophe finally ruinous, for it was not blindly vengeful; but its pardons were not to be had by I did not understand! I did not intend! The requirements of its compassion were inexorable: that a man bear responsibility for the wrong that came through him and be purified of it.

In his case, how else than by silence?

The letter to his mother that he had begun almost two days ago was in the blotter under his folded arms. He took it out and destroyed it.

Are you, my friend, he thought, seeing yourself as the hero of Greek tragedy? You are only a little schoolmaster trying to be honest. You are only a little boaster whose pet melodrama has caught him in a trap.

But there is a health of body that will not let the mind despair, and next morning at breakfast, when Tucker came in with the mail, Sturgess's heart leapt to the unreasoning hope that there might be a letter for him from Valerie. There were four letters from America; none for him with an English stamp; and a wave of disappointment, as unreasoning as his former hope, swept over him. But hope and disappointment were the flow and ebb of life, not the flat, tideless negation of yesterday. He was no longer numb; pain returned, an animating flood of sensual desolation; and the idea that he might see her again to-night, and hear and touch her, isolated itself from all other ideas, and burned him.

"Philip," Julian said.

The tone, peremptory but exceedingly quiet, compelled Sturgess from a profound abstraction. He moved his head with a jerk of alarm as he might have done if he had been shouted at in a half-sleep. Julian was stiff in his chair, his eyes almost shut, his left wrist and hand flattened upon the papers before him, as though he had covered them suddenly and were holding them down.

"Something has happened that ought not to have happened."

"What has happened?"

"The fool Tucker dealt a letter of yours into my pile. It is from Valerie Barton. I have read only the signature and the postscript. But I have read them."

Sturgess stretched out his hand for the letter. "Then I expect there's no harm done."

"I have more to say," Julian answered without moving. "A snapshot fell out of the letter. I saw it inevitably. In the postscript she says that, remembering what happened on Radlett's Island and how much you and she have spoken of him, she sends you a photograph of her brother. . . . There it is. There is the letter." He pushed them across the table and waited.

Sturgess read without speaking. The letter was very short and changed nothing. It had as its only purpose not to be silent and to say good-bye without bitterness.

"Well, Julian?"

Instead of speaking, as Sturgess had expected, of the tragic error they had made together, of Heron's innocence and death, Julian demanded: "How much does she know?"

The question was so astonishing and, in a sense, so shocking that Sturgess did not at once answer, and Julian repeated: " How much does Valerie Barton know? "

" No more than she did. That her brother is gone, presumed dead."

" But that Heron was her brother——"

" No."

" Then why did you say that you were sure she would not dine here to-night? "

The conversation was moving in a direction that Sturgess did not understand.

" Why, in heaven's name, do you ask that? What does it matter? You look at a photograph which tells you that the man we killed was a loyal officer, and all you ask is how much Valerie knows and why she should not dine here! Isn't that a purely personal matter between her and me? "

" I have known for nearly four years," Julian answered, " that we were mistaken. As soon as I reached England, I sent for Lang's *dossier*. It tallied beyond question. I have seen that photograph before."

" And you wouldn't tell me? "

" I have told no one."

Sturgess was hot with anger. " But when you saw what was happening between Valerie and me, surely, if you are not inhuman, your precious rule of secrecy——"

" Listen," Julian interrupted, " get this straight. That Heron was genuine I have known for four years. That he was her brother I have just learned. The name of Barton didn't appear in the *dossier*. The next-of-kin was down as Lang, a younger brother — presumably the one now in South Africa. That I remember because, when the Brussels story got through to London and I had supplemented it, there was a high-level decision on how much should be told. Obviously, no purpose could be served, and much harm might be done, by telling the next-of-kin about Brussels and the River Line. Finally, Heron was reported as having escaped from his prison — there were other ways of knowing that — and as missing afterwards. . . . The names of Lang and Barton didn't link in my mind until three minutes ago. That was new. You have to accept that or we shall talk at cross-purposes."

"Yes, Julian. . . . I accept it. . . . I'm sorry I flared up," Sturgess answered dully and helplessly; then added: "My God, you and Marie must have thought me a pretty fool! Coming here, all agog to chatter about our 'Blaise adventure' and understanding not the first thing — the very first thing — about it! There was I, the complete fool, rather proud of myself for having been 'professional' enough to save the River Line from an enemy agent and to kill the man who—" He broke off in shame and indignation. "And there were you and Marie smiling at me up your sleeves, letting me babble on, allowing me day after day——"

"Steady!" Julian exclaimed.

"Well, isn't it so?"

"No."

"Anyhow you saw fit not to tell me — you and Marie."

"I couldn't tell you. . . . And Marie has nothing to do with it." Julian leaned across the table, taut with anxiety. "At any moment, Marie may walk in through that door and say good-morning and begin to pour out coffee. If she does, keep your mouth shut." He stretched out his hand towards the photograph, which lay face upward between them, and covered it with his palm. The downward pressure drove back the blood from his finger-nails. "Put that away, Philip. Now — put it away!"

He lifted his hand; but Sturgess instead of returning the photograph to its envelope, slid it across the corner of the table: " Take it. Do what you like with it."

Julian drew it towards him and held it, beside his plate, under his hand.

" I'm sorry to be excitable," he said, returning with an effort of will to his ordinary calm, " but to see that photograph lying about shakes me."

" Are you telling me that Marie still believes that Heron was false ? "

" Yes."

" Knowing yourself that he was genuine, you have kept her in ignorance for over four years ? "

Julian shook his head. " It hasn't been four years. You forget: I had no communication with her from the night we left Blaise until the war ended. When I did make contact again, it became clear to me that she didn't know. I had thought she would. Obviously, after we had gone, she would have sent back a report to River Line headquarters and I assumed that by that time they would have had the truth from England and have told her. But it seems not. Either they hadn't the truth themselves, at any rate before she was captured, or, for reasons of discipline — or perhaps for reasons of mercy, they chose not to tell it to her. Those secret communication networks didn't work easily. They were used for executive orders, not for post-mortem chatter. Even if headquarters knew and intended to tell her, that particular message would have had no sort of priority."

" And yet," Sturgess said, " we know that she did receive a negative report from the cryptographers on Heron's letter."

" She did indeed," Julian replied. " It was her telling me that in the way she told it which gave me warning that she knew nothing else. I confess I had more or less taken it for granted, when I found her in Switzerland, that she would know as much as I did, but I didn't rush my fences. There she was, propped up in bed with black rings round her eyes and with wrists and hands so horribly emaciated that — well, I can assure you, the whole subject of Heron's death wasn't one for me to plunge into. And anyhow," he added with the first smile that had appeared on his face since the photograph had fallen out of its envelope, " as you know, Philip — you have reproved me for it often enough — I have a habit of not being the first to talk. So I held my hand and left her to lead. . . . She didn't lead. She talked about Heron, always with affection, as one does speak lovingly and calmly and unpassionately of the dead. She talked of him a great deal in her own special way, as somebody who had to die but was completely exempt from our judgment — somebody above the battle; but she gave not a hint of knowing that she and you and I had been wrong. So I still held my hand. She, too, can be reticent, and it seemed to me possible that she might be biding her time. But gradually it dawned on me that she really didn't know, and it seemed wanton cruelty to tell her — anyhow then. I postponed. I went on postponing. While she was so damnably weak and ill, I wouldn't tell. When she got better and began to be happy again, I couldn't. When she — but that's our own sentimental history."

Sturgess heard him to the end, tried to answer and failed.

" Are you blaming me, Philip ? "

" No. . . . The cases are different."

" What cases ? "

" Your marrying, and my — not asking."

Julian was egoist enough for this to come upon him

with fresh impact. "Tell me," he said, and Sturgess told him of what had happened on Radlett's Island. When the little story was done, Julian said:

"But you will ask her?"

"No, Julian."

"Nor tell her?"

"Wouldn't that be towards her what you said it would be towards Marie — 'wanton cruelty'?"

"If you and she love each other, it is a thousand times more cruel not to ask her to marry you. You are mad, Philip."

"No," Sturgess answered steadily. "You are talking of what you don't know or understand. If you think, you will see that I am not mad — or even stubborn or stupidly quixotic. Do you suggest that I should marry without telling her?"

Julian hesitated. "I did."

"And have lived in terror — or half-terror — ever since. Isn't that true?"

"We have lived together. She has been happy, I think."

The grateful patience and gentleness with which those words were spoken came from Julian so unexpectedly and cast so revealing a light on the difficult and sensitive adaptations of his marriage, that Sturgess, suddenly and deeply moved, stood up and walked clear of the table, passing behind Julian's chair.

"She is happy. I give you that."

Julian glowed in the reassurance. "It's good to hear you say it. . . . And you, Philip? Why is it impossible that you——"

"For the moment," Sturgess said, "leave me out. Your case and mine are different. You and Marie at least share responsibility for what was done——"

" No," Julian broke in vehemently, " there you are wrong. You miss the whole point. If Marie knew, she would see the whole responsibility as hers. It was my knife, but it was her order."

How bitterly consistent! Sturgess thought. Even now, even in this, the ' professional ' point of view!

" Still," he exclaimed, " the thing is a barrier between you two. I have lived in this house long enough to see and feel it. It's a link also. Heron brought you together and binds you together — and yet your secrecy about him keeps you apart."

Julian sat unmoving on his chair, his hand still pressed down over the photograph, and seemed scarcely to be listening.

" Are you content," Sturgess continued, " to go on like this for ever? Always afraid that some poor fool like me will blurt it out? "

" Who could but you yourself? Frewer is dead."

" Always afraid, then, to talk to her of the one subject which, because you daren't speak of it, grows bigger and bigger in your mind? Is that possible? "

Without looking at him, Julian murmured: " It hasn't proved impossible yet."

" Happy? "

" In one way, yes. . . . In another—"

The sentence was too bitter to be finished. A grey look of frustration and endurance came over Julian's face. Sturgess swung a chair round and straddled it, leaning his forearms on its back.

" Even if Marie did assume the whole responsibility, isn't she strong enough? "

" Ah," Julian replied in a tone of fierce retaliation, " isn't that a question you had better ask yourself? It needs courage to take risks with other people's lives.

More than with your own. It needs a courage which — quiet ! "

The door behind Sturgess opened and Marie came in. He was in the chair she ordinarily used at breakfast. When he had risen and given it to her, he went back round the table to his own place, where he found cold coffee in his cup and began to drink it.

" No letters ? " she asked.

" None for you," Julian said, and turned the handles of the coffee-pot and the milk-jug towards her. Then, with no alteration in his voice, with all emotion drained out of it, he said : " But this came, you had better see it."

She looked at the photograph, not at first with visible shock but with searching interest. The colour mounted in her face ; then receded and receded.

" He was an officer of the Hussars," Julian said, seeming to think that she had not understood. " He was an English officer. You had better know."

She took her hands from the table and folded them in her lap.

" Oh, Julian ! . . . So terribly long ! " And her arms and shoulders began to tremble. Afraid for her, Sturgess half-rose from his chair, but Julian, who was nearer, did not stir.

" Poor Julian," she said, " is this new to you ? "

" No, Marie. I ought to have told you long ago. I—"

She raised her head and thrust back her hair as though she were letting a burden fall. " My dearest, it is not new to me."

28

AGAINST Sturgess's expectations, a message delivered during the forenoon offered Mrs. Muriven's excuses for not dining that evening but added that Valerie would come alone. The news caused in him at first a wild lift of the heart, for he had settled into the belief that in all his life he would not see her again; but delight ebbed. She was coming, he saw, in the same spirit in which her letter had been written: an unwillingness that the end between them should be, or seem to be, violent or extreme. It was in her character and discipline to behave as she would have behaved if nothing untoward had happened, so that their parting should be made with the least hurt to him and without failure of courage in herself.

During the long day he had more than enough opportunity to observe the new happiness that had come to Marie and Julian. The old constraint was gone; one would have said that they had fallen in love for the first time if there had not been in all their words and looks, and in their being in a room together, a confident ease that there is not in the first tensions of love; and he knew, from their kindness towards him, that they were as conscious as he of the bleakness of his own heart and of the accent of exile which their happiness laid upon it. They did their utmost to draw him in, and he so to respond that no shadow should be cast by him upon their day; but there are delights and sadnesses that will not keep company, and when, in the early afternoon, Marie, seeing him with a walking-stick, said untruthfully that she had no work that might not wait and would come with him, he grasped her hand and shook his head and said: "No, my dear: better alone," and went off without her.

There is no loneliness that so disintegrates the imagination as that which springs from the renouncement of love still within reach. She who has been put away glows retrievably; her warmth continues just beyond the boundary of touch; the remembering fingers, half-deceived, close upon the air where her hand is not; the small beauties of earth — the gleam of a pebble, the sculpture of an oak-twig, the folding-over of grasses under a change of breeze — look out anonymously, like blinded eyes, because she is not present to share those recognitions which divide life from death. This sunshaft might have fallen upon her cheek, this dapple of beech-shadow have streamed away from her shoulders like a cloak as she moved; in this silence her voice would have spoken. Out of her absence, arise, like ghosts, the unending futureless hours, the unlived life dead without burial, a life that cries out to be lived or ended, and has in the mind no grave where it may rest.

He sat down among the trees and covered his face. Memory summoned to him, in disarray, incidents of the days just gone and fragments of them, moods and visions then sacred in their personal validity, presented now as pathetic or absurd, thrown out for the curs of satire to root in: to them the garbage of romance, their natural food. With the eyes of these smart scavengers, he saw his own Unique rotted into their Commonplace, his faith snouted by their avid ridicule. What great words he had flourished then — the very words they mocked at — believing that his own experience was proof against the sneerers at life!

Now he was tricked, and self-tricked, and they were justified.

He knew precisely what argument they would use, commenting on his story. They, the satirical materialists, would say that his problem did not exist, that it was a delusion sprung from a delusion. The dead man, to them, was a rotted carcase, not a presiding spirit; and he himself and she, though alive, were carcases also, differing from the dead only in their possession of appetites. There was, then, no problem or should be none, because there were neither dedications nor values. Whether or not he told her that he was responsible for her brother's death was unimportant because he and she and her brother were dressed-up animals in a disintegrating civilization, and had no spiritual identities extending beyond the limits of physical life. Individual responsibility was, therefore, no more than a phrase because love was only an expression of collective appetite, and love could not be more than this because immortality itself was delusion. There was, then, in the materialists' view, nothing but romantic falseness in his supposing that the present was impregnated by the past and that his marriage to Valerie was prohibited by Heron's death.

Nevertheless it was for him prohibited. Marie herself had at first been able to understand this only if she substituted her reasoning for his intuition; even so, in the little library to which he had retreated from the breakfast-room, she had tried to persuade him to allow her to tell Valerie. She had seen that Valerie, if told the truth, might find it intolerable to be his wife, but this, she had said, was a decision that the girl must be enabled to make for herself; she ought, therefore, to be told. But he had answered that the question was not whether the marriage would seem "tolerable" or "intolerable" to

Valerie; the prohibition, as he felt it, was absolute; because its origin was in Heron himself it could have been lifted only by him. " My responsibility is to him, Marie. My debt, not repayable. He alone might have pardoned it." Marie had looked at him then long and searchingly. " You are binding yourself to the dead," she had answered, and he had replied: " I don't feel it so. He is always alive for me — here above all. From the first evening in this house — in his place at your table; among us, on your lawn. And quite unspeakably alive *in her*: her voice, her movement, the carriage of her head!" It was then that Marie had accepted what, until then, she had, for his sake, struggled against. " Ah, my poor Philip, if it is in *her* you see him, then I have no more to say."

Over and over again, within the darkness of his hands or as he looked out through the wood at the benign sky, memories of argument and sensation pursued him with their vain repetitions and wasted delights, leading him always in that dreadful circle which, when it is called sleeplessness, at least has a centre in sleep and purpose in the longing for it — like starlings, hovering and circling, which will gather and come to rest at last before their long flight. But his confusion had not even the sleepless longing; his circle had no centre. The starlings would dip and hover and cross endlessly, the earth withdrawn from under them; no rest for thought, only hovering and falling, and falling through trackless space, wide awake and staring at the pitilessly benign sky.

So it seemed as he sat there; but clocks continue, the plain obligations of existence, hateful though they appear to be, can bring a kind of comfort. You bath and shave though the heavens fall, write cheques, answer letters, and so behave in company that others may not be embarrassed. You don't sit on in a wood so late that your hosts begin to wonder what has become of you; and Sturgess began his return journey in good time: down through the wood until the path opened out to a view of the lawn.

On that Sunday evening when he and Marie had come home by this way — the evening of the Roman snail — Julian, waiting for them on the lawn, had known instantly that they had been talking of Heron; and Sturgess went to the place where Julian had been standing, and stood there.

Quiet came upon him. The wheels of his agitation paused. It was as though he had been standing at cross-roads in an angry city and had looked up to find only earth and sky. He stood there, not only without physical movement, but in a deepening stillness, which was almost a cancellation, of the self he had hitherto recognized as his own, a shedding of the fret and triviality of his consciousness like the falling away of a dress that had entangled him. His saying to Marie that "Heron was always alive for him" — by which he had meant, when he spoke it, that he was imaginatively aware of Heron's bodily character and, particularly, of Valerie's physical resemblance to her brother — seemed now to be inadequate and shallow, almost to be untrue; Heron was present in a different sense, in an identity not related to his appearance when in the flesh; but Sturgess did not yet know what this meant, he knew only that his earlier thoughts had been inadequate; he reached out toward the new concept of identity — of Heron's and of his own — as one reaches out through the music of poetry towards a meaning not yet grasped; and he fell away from it peacefully, without a sense of frustration.

A few minutes later, as he entered the house, the

experience seemed to have receded so far that it was no longer his. It continued in him only as a story might, which had been told him long ago and impressed his imagination with its essential truth, but the substance of which he had forgotten.

29

When he was ready for dinner and came downstairs, he found Marie alone on the porch as he had on his first evening in the house. Though he had passed beyond curiosity about the events at Blaise, he desired to speak of Heron with the same desire that one has to open the window of a room too long shut, and he asked her what had happened when she entered her father's room. What had he said? What had convinced her of Heron's guilt?

" I was not convinced of it," she answered. " But I wasn't convinced, either, of his innocence. Father was in a condition of extreme, suppressed excitement — for him it was as if the prophecies of his whole life had been fulfilled. Even if he had been capable of going through the evidence piece by piece, I couldn't have sat down to listen; time had run out. I was told about the letter, and that other evidence existed — a long chain of it — which culminated in the letter, and by which all of you——"

" All of us ? " Sturgess broke in.

" Father said ' They '. He said that ' They ' had sent you down from the granary; that ' They ' thought or ' They ' believed. . . . Probably he believed it; certainly I did; it didn't occur to me that you were acting alone; I assumed that your conclusion was Julian's also, perhaps Frewer's too. It was a judgment I couldn't neglect. Heron had come in from Germany without credentials; the verdict on him from Brussels was a dangerously open one; and though my own intuition was against your judgment, it was an intuition I couldn't yield to—" She hesitated before adding: " For personal reasons, and — and because, Philip, even my own intuition in his favour wasn't complete. Do you remember the evening when Heron wanted to come out with me — the evening when Julian arrived? At the time, I was utterly unsuspicious. I thought he wanted to come with me for my sake — and I was right, I suppose. That's the irony of it. . . . But on the last night, when Father was talking to me and I had my decision to make and make instantly, the memory of Heron's attempt to come out with me worked, quite suddenly, the *other* way. I thought I had been *naïve*; it's one of the weaknesses of being my kind of intellectual that one is afraid of being *naïve*, one is suspicious of truth when it is simple. I thought that I'd been flattering myself about his wish to come with me for my sake, and so — do you understand that? — memory swung round, I saw its other face, it worked the other way."

She was silent, looking at him with a sudden, deep curiosity. " I wonder — is that what you would call a feminine reaction? I think the same thing would have happened to you, though for different reasons. . . .

" Not that it makes any odds," she continued, " except the irony of it. . . . I thought I had deceived myself about his wanting to come with me for my sake, and that steeled me. But neither that, nor your evidence, nor my father's passionate conviction, convinced me. I wasn't convinced. I was no more ' convinced ' than the captain of a ship who sees a vast menace come at him out of a fog, and has to act instantly without full knowledge. I had to act — or shirk. There could be no pause for investigation. In face of the evidence I couldn't conceivably leave Heron alone, alive and unguarded, nor could I let him go on to the Spanish frontier. And to have cancelled your going then, to have left Félix stranded, to have blocked my end of the Line, would have cost more lives than one. What I did I had to do. There wasn't an alternative. On the evidence I had then, and under the same pressure of time, I would do now what I did then."

Sturgess made no comment. Her tone, clipped, decisive, studiously impersonal, told him so much of the suffering which she would not allow herself to elaborate or to pity, that he deliberately let her words fall away into a long silence.

" You said something that surprised me," he said at last. " Talking of your belief that you had been *naïve* and that, after all, you had been wrong in thinking that Heron had wanted to come out with you for your own sake, you said that the same thing would have happened to me. . . . Why to me ? "

" You are *naïf*, Philip. I am not. One can be deceived both ways."

" My mother says ' guileless '," he answered with a smile.

She glanced at him. " I wonder whether you have ever asked yourself why people are fond of you — people quite different from one another and worlds apart from you. . . . Or why, if it comes to that, Valerie loves you. She does, you know."

" Yes," he said firmly, " I know. At least——"

" No," she cried, " don't qualify it ! One knows that it is so or that it is not. One knows by the touch of a hand, the feel of the air. I knew that Heron did not love me. And you know that Valerie——"

" Very well," he answered, " I won't qualify."

" But do you know why she loves you ? Do you in the least know what is lovable in you ? It is the fact that you *don't* know. You are loved because, in that respect, you are without vanity. The miracle happens because, to you, it is always a miracle. People are desired who expect to be desired, and envied who expect to be envied, but no one is ever truly and deeply loved who is not as incredulous of love as he is of death. I shall never be greatly loved because my intellect is too quick, I am not *naïve* enough; for the same reason, my father, poet though he was, must always have fallen short of being a supreme poet; his poetry never took his own breath away. He wasn't ever incredulous of what appeared on his paper. He knew precisely how it came there. He knew the reason for everything; so do I — even for love, and so I shall never be loved as you are loved, and I shall never — oh, well, let it go. . . . Look, she has walked up through the wood."

" Say what you were going to say, Marie."

" Shall I? Very well." And she added with the self-protective stiffness of a teacher announcing the solution of a problem: " I shall never be loved as you are loved by that girl walking towards us now, and I shall never know how to die as Heron died. Do you understand that? "

" No."

" I have not wonder enough. It is the grace to receive Grace. Not granted to me. Do you understand that? "

" Perhaps," he said, and would have struggled dutifully on. " I understand——"

" Ah," she exclaimed under her breath, " don't try. Don't have the killing vanity to try. That is my own intellectual sin."

30

When Valerie was among them, they sat in the porch for a little while and drank sherry there before going into dinner. The stress, eased in practice by the discipline of good manners, was less than Sturgess had feared. They talked first of Mrs. Muriven, of the reasons for her not having come; then, in the dining-room, of Valerie's journey, of her brother in South Africa, of the conditions of life she would find there.

"To what extent have you imagined them?" Julian asked. "I mean have you, in your own mind, a picture of any of the rooms or of the view from a window?" and they began to discuss the seemingly contradictory truth that one can imagine a place without having formed a describable picture of it.

"Just as in reading history or in turning over the pages of an old letter, one gets often a clear idea of a person without having a notion whether he was bearded or clean-shaven or what was the colour of his eyes," Julian said. "A place or a person can have being in our minds without having physical existence there. Which, on the face of it, is odd."

Sturgess confessed that often, when reading a novel, though he fully accepted the author's descriptions, he at the same time saw the action move among the scenes of his childhood, and this without any sense of incongruity or anachronism, but rather with reinforcement of the writer's evocative power. "The writers who are dead for me are those who either don't set me off on that private track at all or who drag me away from it and tie me down by insisting on physical appearances overmuch — writers, I mean, who don't enable me or won't allow me to imagine for myself. It's as if the writer of a ghost-story were to tell me that the ghost was seven feet four inches high and was wrapped in a sheet."

It was spoken lightly enough. They seemed to be skimming the surface of the problem of imagination that Julian had so casually raised. But below that surface was the related question of identity's independence of physical character, and Sturgess, while he spoke and played his part, as best he could, in keeping their discussion easily impersonal, felt that he was being drawn down below the surface of his words and theirs; that the room and the tensions of thought in the room were changing.

There seemed to be two conversations in progress: that of words, struggling for imperfect metaphor and blurred by the perpetual inadequacy of language; and that of intuitions, a communication lucid and direct, as though they four seated at that table, separated beings, were really beginning to speak to one another under their divided breath.

It was no more than a hint, but a hint in the same kind with Sturgess's experience in the garden. It re-awoke in him, not a mental picture of Heron alive or dead, but a sense of being penetrated by that steadfast radiance of spirit, or equanimity, which *was* Heron. The influence remained upon him like a fragrance, a part of the breath of his mind, long after he had ceased to take separate account of it, and dinner was over and they had gone out on to the lawn.

Seated there, looking out over the valley, speaking little himself and listening to the voices of the others, he understood that the evening was entered on its last period. Hitherto there had always been barriers, comforting in their postponements, between him and his final parting from her, and the evening had stretched out before him as a book stretches out while any whole chapter, however brief, has yet to be begun, and as life stretches out until the mind says abruptly: this is my death-bed. He had been able to say to himself: she will come and we shall talk together in the porch, and after that we shall go in across the hall, and after that she will be opposite me at dinner, visible, audible, within reach, while Tucker in his white jacket fusses slowly round the table and the light moves over the walls; and after that there will be the period called "after dinner" before she rises from her chair and says: now I really think I must be going home, and the little delays of parting — the last look at the valley, the going into the house for a scarf or a wrap — begin.

Now there were no more barriers. In an hour, two perhaps, she would gather her bag from her lap, and rise. They would all rise and she would say — Then she would be gone and the future have slid over its precipice. He would say good-night to Marie; Julian would offer him a last drink which he would accept so that the day might not end, so that the day might not end; and he would go to his bedroom and shut the door carefully and firmly because it had a defective latch. Then . . .

But the last period was not ended. There was still an hour.

The sun, declining amid patches of cumulus towards the high wood where Sturgess had spent that afternoon, thrust a long dagger of gold down the valley's eastward-looking slope and wiped his blade along its ridges. Over the opposite hill above Tarryford the web of twilight, woven first on the river's bank, was drawn slowly upward. A herd of cattle on low ground, which a moment earlier had glowed like brass on the intense green of that moulded earth, faded; the earth under them flattened; and inch by inch the roots, the trunks, the branches of the trees above were flooded by the mounting dusk. As yet the upper ranges of elm and oak held a liquid fire, and seemed, at their translucent edge, to diffuse it, as a nimbus, against the steadily reflecting sky. Soon they too would be gone but there was a moment when, it seemed, evening was poised between sunshine and dusk, and birds and men and the beasts of the field waited and watched, and the pulse of time was still.

They were silent then, an interval falling in their conversation, as though with natural awe and by common consent with the birds and beasts and the quiet earth they acknowledged themselves to be creatures. He watched her for her beauty that he might in the years to come a little remember it, and, as he watched, there came to him from within her an interior grace, hers because she was the lamp that gave it out, yet not hers only. Of this enduring light, seen through men and things and yet not part of them, as light is not part of a lamp, he became aware through her, who was alive and within reach of his hand, as he had been aware of it a few hours earlier through Heron who was invisible; and for an instant the distinctions between physical presence and physical absence were burned away in his mind, and creation shone singly. Even when the experience again receded from him because he was not trained to accept it and grapple it to him, the sense of it remained in his sense of its having passed, as though he had touched the hem of a garment.

So it happened that when she began to speak of her brother — not of her brother in South Africa, but of her brother who was dead, and when she spoke of Heron also as though he and her brother had been two, not one, he did not feel any stress until he saw it in the faces of the others. Then, like one who wakes from a dream of supreme simplification to a confused unhappiness in his own life, he became, as they were, perturbed and anxious. It seemed to him terrible and humiliating that she should be in ignorance of what they all knew, and that out of that ignorance she should continue to speak of her brother and of Heron in the presence of those who had killed him.

Marie interrupted her; Julian did his utmost to turn her aside; but in vain.

" He has been in my mind all day," she said, " and this evening more than ever. There will be broken days in London, I know, but they will be full of business, and now on this lawn — this is really my last night in England, the one at any rate that I shall remember as the last. If he had been alive, I shouldn't have been going, and there was a time this morning when I felt that my going was a new separation from him — a kind of desertion. Now I don't feel that but much more as if——"

In her hesitation, she looked at Sturgess expectantly with Heron's wide, straight eyes.

" As if," he suggested, speaking under compulsion, " he were here ? "

" That," she answered, " and more, even, than that." Then she turned with embarrassment to Julian. " I'm sorry. It must be tiresome of me to speak like this of someone you have never known. Philip and I have talked of him so much that I feel — how I wish you had known him too ! "

She spoke the last phrase suddenly and passionately. Julian winced but made no further attempt to divert her.

" Not," she added, " that the appearance of anyone

matters ultimately, I suppose. Anyhow one can't communicate it. It has always seemed odd to me that one can't. If in my ship, two or three days from now, I were speaking of this evening to some stranger and tried to describe Philip so that the stranger might have a picture of him in his mind, I should fail utterly. The eyes, the mouth, the nose, the shape of the head — yes, all that, all the separate bits, but never the whole appearance recognizably. Language simply doesn't provide."

" Nor does thought," Julian shot out. " Not only will you be unable, two or three nights ahead, to describe Philip's face, but you will be unable to *see* it. Look away now! Look out over the valley! . . . Can you see his face distinctly, clearly, completely, as you do when your eyes are on it? Can you? "

She turned her head away. " I can see *him*! "

" But his face, his features? "

" No," she admitted, " not as one sees with one's eyes. Or even in a photograph. But *him* I can see." She turned back swiftly towards them. " Of course Philip knows what my brother looked like. He has a photograph."

" Marie and I know what he looked like," Julian said.

" You have seen the photograph? "

Marie caught her breath; her lips moved to speak. Sturgess thought she would cry out to end the intolerable deception, but Julian answered steadily: " Yes, Philip showed it to us," and the danger passed.

" I'm glad," Valerie said. " Not that it tells anything. A photograph is like a book which is said to be ' life-like ' but tells nothing — doesn't even try to tell because it doesn't recognize the existence of the man within. But I'm glad, all the same, you have seen it," she said, and there was a little silence.

Sturgess leaned back in his chair, lifted his hands' grip from his knees, and slackened the muscles of his cheeks and mouth — it was a conscious grimace, as though the muscles had stiffened in a freezing wind. The danger that Marie might pour out the truth was past — if there had been a danger. Perhaps there had been none; she was pledged not to speak and was trained to silence.

Valerie was saying that she had for a long time been greatly troubled by the fact that she didn't know how her brother had died — by his having simply " vanished ". She didn't even know in what country — in Germany, perhaps, or Belgium, but she had thought in France.

" Why ? " Julian exclaimed. " What proof was there of that ? "

" Proof? None. . . . Of course, no proof." She had plucked fragments of grass from the lawn. She rubbed them, and let them fall, between her hands. " Not in the least to know how he died," she said, " was for a time a bleak gap in my knowledge of him. It prevented me from being with him imaginatively when he died; there was a kind of brutality in not knowing. Do you understand that? As though I had abandoned him to die alone? I couldn't stop trying to see the place where he died and trying to go to it — sometimes it was a field, sometimes a black muddy street, sometimes it was a brick cell with a bare electric bulb — but it was all false and I knew it inside me; images of loneliness, that was all. Not true with his truth — or my own. . . . And sometimes, as a corrective, I used to imagine that he died among friends, new friends who had learned to know and love him, and that he hadn't the shudder of loneliness when death came. . . ."

" That may have been true," Marie said.

" But that is long ago," Valerie continued as though she had not heard, " that's all past — my trying and trying to picture the scene and visit it."

They listened to her in a silence which became an inability to speak.

" Even if he were killed," she said, " and the men who killed him were watching him die—" but her voice stopped; she was not yet prepared to finish that sentence; and began again, speaking with authority as though she were recounting certainties:

" I was completely wrong. The circumstances of his dying were not, for him, of the least importance; they became what he called ' effects '. Even if he was killed and the men who killed him watched him die—"

Marie's hand slid along the wooden arm of her chair, the fingers curling over its end.

"—there would, I know," the speaker continued, " have been no question of his forgiving or not forgiving them; certainly not of his condemning them. They would have appeared to him as men who at least bore their responsibility in the predicament of the world. He would not have condemned them. As he died, blame and forgiveness too would have appeared to him as ' effects ', things not to be reckoned in judgment, belonging to a plane of reality that he was leaving behind."

She raised her head and waited, and seemed to listen before she drew a long, quiet breath.

" As he died," she said, " I mean, as he found himself being drawn away from *this* into a deeper consciousness underlying it, our ' effects ' evaporated, our debts and credits were — emptied out. He let them go, as one lets sleep go when one wakes or lets waking go when one sleeps, easily and simply, without wrench, without loss — ' loss without losing '. For a moment, between sleeping and waking, he was incredulous that they should go so easily; then, not."

The phrase she had used, Heron's phrase, "loss without losing", she had had, Sturgess knew, through him, but neither by glance nor intonation had she recognized this. She had spoken the words as if they had been a memory altogether hers; and he quite deliberately, knowing the risk, seeing it no longer as a risk to be avoided, but — as he felt it now — compelled to bring to the surface the truth which was so evidently seeking expression in her, asked: "'Loss without losing' — who said that?"

She answered without tremor: "My brother did," but no sooner had she said this than she stirred in her chair and seemed to falter. Her eyes moved inquiringly, then steadied in the watchful gaze of one who has heard the sound of wheels on a road as yet empty. Knowledge approached in her eyes; Sturgess saw it there before her own mind could give shape to it.

"Heron did," she said at last as though this were her first reply to his question.

The movement in her chair was now completed; she stood up without taking her eyes from them and remained still with that rare, active stillness, that potentiality of movement, which was Heron's beauty and her own. They rose with her. Beyond her shoulders a light appeared in Julian's workroom and a small, rounded human figure moved to and fro across the long windows of the bay, beginning to pull the curtains across, hesitating, opening them again, so that the window-beam lay down like a carpet over the steps and the path.

Little by little the connexion between the two answers she had given, between Heron and her brother, was visibly made; the identity flowed into her like an indrawn breath, and her whole being, in a sigh of incredulity and acceptance, breathed out the implications of it. She began to look, like a puzzled but not frightened animal, from face to face, as though these faces, newly seen, were looking in upon her own profound and inmost safety. . . . You? . . . And you? . . . And you? . . . And he! . . . But she lay close to her safety, like a bird that is being watched through a hedge.

The plane of the window-light behind her shook, and appeared to slide upward. Julian moved urgently, thinking she would crumple and fall; but she was not falling; she had bent her head suddenly and pressed her face into her hands.

"No," she said gently, putting down her hands. "No. It's only that I am tired."

As they returned to the house small material things appeared to Sturgess in the minuteness and brilliancy with which, sometimes, release from stress endows them, as though Nature, in the illumination of her detail, the offer of her miniatures, were disposed to show tenderness for frightened Man now and then. When he looked back over the valley, which was now a deep trough of darkness curving away southward, even his thought of the river, flowing within that darkness, was of its drops and ripples, as though each had its distinct individuality, its separable history, as it slipped down over pebble or reed, or clung in the cavern of an overhanging bank; and within the house, he was aware, as never before, not of a generalized fragrance, but of tiny, hinting night-scents and sweetnesses drifting in, on distinguishable currents, from the outer air.

The drawing-room was dark when they entered it. A fleeting pallor of hand or face, a murmur of words, a movement of dress, an increasing definition of forms as the bare windows asserted their influence, were all that came to him, but they were now the darting fire-points of perception, that pricking of stars through a night-sky which unroofs the world. Julian put matches into his hand. He felt for the oval chimney of the table-lamp, raised it, watched the little flame run blue along the wick. As the flame turned from blue to yellow and the pleated shade filled with light, he turned back, as it were, from the intense privacies of his own mind into the whole room, where he saw that he and she were alone.

" Would you never have told me ? " she asked.

" No."

The unexplaining word, spoken not abruptly but as thoughtfully as a multitude of reasons, sounded to him clumsy as soon as he had spoken it, but it brought to the corners of her mouth the same smile with which she had once told him that she found his suddenness " exciting ".

" Why ? " she asked.

There were good reasons; those he had given to Marie, to Julian, even to himself: that to have told her wouldn't have mended matters; that the fact would still have stood between them. These reasons he gave her, but they were no longer of importance to him. While he spoke, his mind was working at a deeper level of experience. He had been guilty and now was innocent. He had been imprisoned by the past and now was free. This was what he wished to say to her: that on the lawn, while she spoke and Heron spoke in her, everything . . . had become clear.

Struggling to say this, he sat down beside her on the sofa, took her hands, held them a moment, but let them go.

" Everything became clear " — what meaningless words ! He hated vagueness, above all in himself, and turned away from his own experience on the lawn because an attempt to translate it into speech would make his practical, outward, reasonable self seem false.

"It isn't easy to say," he began.

The form of his thought was that, on the lawn while she was speaking, he had been absolved. Solution of tragedy had come, as solution and absolution must always come, from within tragedy itself. He felt this, but could not yet say it, even in mental words.

"It isn't easy to say," was all he managed to bring out as indication that, amid the "good reasons" he was giving her so industriously, there was an underlying truth that he couldn't yet communicate.

She helped him. "Does it need saying?"

"Yes, it does," he said. "In a way it's the treaty between us." He moved away from her to adjust the wick of the table-lamp. As he stooped over it, with his fingers on the milled edge of its turning-disc, understanding of the whole day through which he had passed flowed into him.

During the day, in the high wood, he had felt himself bound to silence, not by reasons that might be reasoned away, but by an absolute prohibition: had felt that he was held by a grip of moral destiny, as the victims of tragic catastrophe were always held, which was not to be loosened by any rebellion of his or any self-justification or any attempt to repudiate responsibility for the past, or by any act in her of forgiveness or oblivion. To feel this, to be as it were subdued into accepting as just a justice that his reason had not made, contradicted all the prides of his modernism. Hitherto it had been the habit of his mind to suppose that men were responsible only for the foreseeable consequences of their acts. But alone in the wood, he had known that all acts and thoughts were of the spirit as well as of the reason; seeds passing beyond the sower's control as they drifted from his hand, falling into an infinite earth and multiplying there. To rebel against their deep consequences was meaningless, the always frustrated struggle of human contrivance relying upon itself. The solution of tragedy, the averting of catastrophe finally destructive, could come, he had felt, if it came at all, only from within; not by his pardoning himself or by her pardoning him or by their agreeing to disregard the past, but by a redemptive force rising up from within the tragedy itself.

It had arisen. Heron had entered into her and inhabited her. Redemptive power, not of the human will, acting in Heron, had been communicated through her. This was what Sturgess wished to say. He desired passionately to know that she was fully conscious of the experience of which she had been the instrument.

But the language of conversation, even between those who love each other, holds fast to the level of experience for which it was chiefly designed, and when his fingers came away from the milling of the lamp-disc and he turned back to her, it was only to explain once more why he had deliberately concealed the truth from her.

"If," he began, "if, on the island when you showed me the photograph, I had said——"

"Or," she answered, "if I had guessed then—"

An attempt of their wills to cancel the truth by sharing it would have been in vain. The knowledge, if they had relied upon reason to free them from its effect, would have been a locked room in their house. A room that they would at first have agreed to keep locked; then, perhaps, have tried to open. A room, they knew now, that neither could have opened.

"You were right," she said. "We should have been worldly-wise and tolerant. We should have tried every key, I suppose — reason, forgiveness, plain oblivion — and they would have seemed to turn. But the room would still have been locked. . . . You were right," she repeated. " One can't shut one's eyes to things not seen by eyes. . . . As it is——"

" As it is ? "

" Peace, dear Philip."

" Between us ? "

" And between us and him."

At last she had spoken of Heron. It was the recognition that Sturgess longed for, but it was still, for him, incomplete. She spoke, as she had on the lawn, with authority; but how actively, how deeply, was she aware of its origin ? For him, she had *been* Heron : he had been witness not of a vision, but of an interior grace.

" This evening," he said, " when you were letting little pieces of grass fall between your hands. . . . On the lawn—" but he stopped, there being no words for his question.

She too allowed words to deflect her. " I saw nothing and heard nothing."

" Saw ! Heard ! That isn't what I was going to ask ! That precisely is *not* — one doesn't see or hear what is inside oneself."

Then she answered his question.

" Ah," she said, " the rest is true. If you mean that *he* was within me — yes, that is true. And you knew it. That is the treaty between us — and between us and him."

LAUGHARNE and LONDON : 1947–48